"There are times in your life when you know you have to do something," Jessie began.

"You don't understand why. You just know from the bottom of your soul it's the right thing to do. That somehow doing this one thing will change your life forever. And if you miss this chance…" She shivered.

As far-fetched and vague as her explanation seemed, David sensed it was the most honest thing she'd revealed all night.

"I need to watch Isabel." She spoke softly, but with a conviction anchored in solid rock.

After a long silence, David agreed. "Okay. It's settled. She's thriving under your care, and that's what counts."

When she exhaled, he inhaled her breath. In that exact moment he felt something shift within his soul. He couldn't put his finger on it. David knew only that for the first time in too long he felt alive. He felt hope. And her smile scared him to death.

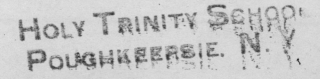

Books by Crystal Stovall

Love Inspired

With All Josie's Heart #126
A Groom Worth Waiting For #155
Gifts of Love #170

CRYSTAL STOVALL

dreamed of writing inspirational romances from the moment she discovered Grace Livingston Hill's novels as a teenager. These books changed her life in a profound way, starting her on a quest to blend faith and romance in her personal life, as well as launching her writing career. She's a graduate of Oral Roberts University and a recipient of the Romance Writers of America's Golden Heart Award and the Oklahoma Writers' Federation Best Novel Award.

Crystal lives in Tulsa with her husband, Jim, who is president of the Emmy Award-winning Narrative Television Network. Though she's lived in Oklahoma for twenty years, she's still an Easterner at heart. Her frequent visits to her upstate New York hometown—especially a certain boulder on the edge of Cayuga Lake—provide her with the inspiration and perspective that she finds essential to her writing.

Gifts of Love
Crystal Stovall

Love Inspired®

Published by Steeple Hill Books™

STEEPLE HILL BOOKS

Steeple
Hill™

ISBN 0-373-87177-5

GIFTS OF LOVE

Visit us at www.steeplehill.com

Printed in U.S.A.

Cast your bread upon the waters,
for after many days you will find it again.
—*Ecclesiastes* 11:1

To Barbara Ankrum, Barbara Joel, Karen Crane, Jolie Kramer and Debbi Quattrone.

Your friendship is a gift I treasure.

Chapter One

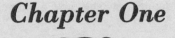

"Oh, Lord," Jessie cried out. "What should I do?"

Forced to make a quick decision, she cried out for protection as she raced down the highway toward her home. But as the rain fell harder, the sky grew darker and visibility drastically decreased.

Verging on panic, Jessie turned on the car radio to a weather report for Springfield, Missouri. As she'd feared, a tornado warning had been issued. Several small twisters had already been spotted within a few miles of her location, and Doppler radar showed the conditions were right for the formation of cells slightly to her south and west. As she passed the highway intersection that the meteorologist had just given as a reference point, Jessie swallowed hard, certain she was in the wrong place at the wrong time.

From deep within her soul, she heard God's answer to her earlier plea and knew what she should do. She had to get out of the car. Immediately. Suddenly, everything Jessie had learned from the meteorologists came flooding back. She was just reaching for her cellular telephone to let her parents know where she was, when something to the west caught her eye. Looking out, she saw a funnel over the distant field.

Without another thought, Jessie parked the car on the side of the road and threw the strap of her purse over her head. In a flash of lightning, she spotted a highway overpass ahead. Unless her mind was playing tricks, she thought she'd seen the silhouette of a man. Thunder boomed, and she ran as fast as she could.

When her shoes sank into the soft highway shoulder, she left them behind. Reaching the overpass, she saw an outstretched hand and grabbed on to the life preserver God had sent her. She let the strong hand pull her to safety as she gasped for breath. She collapsed against the strong chest without hesitation. Never had she been so glad to see another person.

She caught her breath, realizing she was in the arms of a stranger. Yet, she was too afraid to inch free of his protective touch. Not until a tiny hand patted her head in sync with a soft coo did she realize the man held a child in his arms.

Lifting her head, Jessie met a pair of dark eyes

that reflected the same terror she felt. She was certain she knew this man from somewhere.

Offering a nervous smile, Jessie grasped the child's hand and was surprised by how cold her tiny fingers were. The man's arms tightened around the shivering toddler as he tried to warm her.

"It was a beautiful, bright, sunny day when we left home this morning. I didn't think to pack her sweater," he explained, his voice brimming with frustration and self-blame.

Yanking off her thin sweater, she draped it over the child's shoulders. Though the cotton was damp from the rain and didn't entirely cover the child's legs, she knew it had made a difference when she heard, "Mama, mama..."

For just a second, Jessie forgot she was in the middle of a severe storm as she listened to the precious chatter. *Mama, mama*—these were words she'd believed she might never hear from a child's lips.

With a beholden shine in his eyes, the man said, "I'm David Akers, and this is my daughter, Isabel."

"Of course," Jessie said, relieved to know she hadn't jumped into the arms of a total stranger. "I'm Jessie Claybrook. I think our parents are friends."

"Don and Helene's daughter."

Jessie nodded. "Isn't it a small world?"

"It sure is." Then David turned to more urgent

matters. "Were you listening to the radio? What was the last weather report you heard?"

"We're right in the path of a major storm system. Just as I left the car I saw a funnel in the west. It must have skipped over us or turned direction—otherwise it would have hit by now."

David sighed. "I wish we had a portable radio. From this cubbyhole, I can't see enough."

Wedged into a small pocket beneath the highway which crossed overhead, Jessie felt safe from the pounding rain. At least for the moment.

"I could ease down the embankment," she suggested, understanding David would have if he weren't holding Isabel.

"No, you stay put."

Then Jessie remembered her cellular telephone. For an instant she felt a ray of hope, but the all-circuits-busy signal instantly dashed that.

As Jessie dropped the telephone back into her purse, she saw David's lips move, even felt the warmth of his breath on her neck as he leaned closer, but whatever he'd said was lost in the roar of the wind. Bombarded by unyielding gusts, gritty dirt stung their exposed skin and made it difficult to breathe. They heard a grumble in the distance that sounded like a train coming around a mountain. Instinctively, the trio pressed together as the storm raged. Then, suddenly, all was quiet.

Minutes passed before either Jessie or David moved.

Slowly easing apart, they listened for confirmation that the funnel had dissipated. Not even thunder or lightning dared to pierce the silence, and even the rain fell lightly.

Jessie listened to David's mumbled prayer: *"Please, Lord, I know You and I aren't on great terms these days, but please don't let anything happen to my baby before we get home. I can't lose her, too."*

Unaware Jessie had overheard his plea, David sighed with relief and then matter-of-factly announced, "I think it's over."

"But is it safe to move?" Jessie challenged.

Unwilling to take any unnecessary chances, they waited a few more minutes before edging down the embankment. They saw broken tree limbs scattered across both lanes when they reached the highway shoulder, as well as slack power lines clinging to leaning creosote poles.

"That was some storm," David said, as Isabel held on tightly to his neck.

"Thank God we're okay. And while I'm sorry you and your daughter were caught in the storm, I'm glad I didn't have to tough this one out alone."

"I didn't do much, but I'm glad we made a difference."

Uncertain as to whether it was safe to drive, Jessie

looked to the sky for answers. The growing brightness seemed to give a go-ahead signal. Still, she feared leaving the overpass, leery of what she might encounter down the road.

As if he'd read her thoughts, David asked, "Would you like me to follow you back into town?"

Jessie pressed her hand against her chest with relief. "Normally, I'm not this skittish, but this storm's really unnerved me. It'd mean a lot to know I've got company on the highway."

"Then, it's settled," David said, though he continued to study the sky.

Like her, he seemed unwilling to end this brief encounter.

But Isabel had other ideas. "Mama, mama..." she said, with one finger wedged in the corner of her lip.

Jessie instantly felt the blush on her face. What had she been thinking? David obviously had a wife to go home to.

"We should go," she said. "I'm sure your wife is eager to know you're safe. You're welcome to borrow my cell phone to call her...." Her words trailed off to a hoarse whisper, as anguish streaked across David's face. "I'm sorry. I've made assumptions that are none of my business."

She languished in the uncomfortable silence before he found his voice. "Please...you couldn't know. My wife died a few weeks after Isabel's birth.''

Jessie gazed at the little girl, her heart breaking over such a tragic loss.

David took another look at the sky and said, ''I think we'd better go.''

''Thanks again,'' Jessie said, extending her hand. When David's fingers closed around hers, she felt his warmth and kindness and wished they didn't have to part.

''I'm just glad we're okay.'' As he walked toward his car, he called out, ''Listen, if you're ever at the Hot & Fresh Deli, stop in. A sandwich and a cup of coffee are on the house. I'm the owner.''

''It's a deal,'' Jessie said, turning toward her own car.

But before she could even open the door, the punishing rain and gusting wind started again. Anxious, she glanced back toward David—and that's when she saw the menacing funnel in the distance.

Without hesitation, she raced back to the overpass, meeting David and Isabel. Together they scurried up the embankment until they touched the underside of the crossing highway.

''Hold on to the ledge,'' David shouted above the wind, and Jessie quickly followed his lead, gripping the rough concrete. With Isabel sandwiched between them, she prayed with all her heart that the tornado would leap over them, or lose its power as the last one had.

But it wasn't to be. Sounding like a jet, the twister charged toward them. The wind became so fierce that Jessie didn't know if she could hold on, let alone breathe, as loose gravel and dirt swirled around her.

She lost all concept of time, feeling as if the unmerciful gusts would last forever. Only when lightning flashed could she see David and Isabel.

Oh, Lord, she prayed, *don't desert us now.*

With her arms tiring, Jessie didn't know how much longer she could hang on. But it was for Isabel that she found her strength, because pressed against David's side she helped form a barrier that sheltered the toddler.

Though it seemed impossible, the winds grew stronger, and Jessie felt as if the three of them were trapped in a vacuum. The temperature continued to drop, and she shook as much from the damp air as she did from fear. With her arm muscles stretched until they hurt and her palms rubbed raw from holding on to the concrete ledge, she just didn't know if she could last another second.

Then lightning cracked, and in the bright flash she met David's gaze for just an instant, finding strength in his courage and determination. She wouldn't let him down.

Suddenly, something shifted. She heard him

scream. His body moved. He no longer touched her. The lightning flashed again, and the terror on his face shocked her. He'd purposely positioned himself so as to absorb the brunt of the wind, and now the wind was winning the battle.

"Isabel!" he screamed.

Though she couldn't see clearly in the dusty darkness, she knew he was slipping away. When the lightning flashed again, Jessie saw David lose his grip, letting go first of the ledge and then of Isabel.

With all her might, Jessie fought against the wind, stretching out one arm, grabbing hold of Isabel first by her shirt and then, miraculously, crushing the girl against her chest.

As the lightning cracked again, she looked up and realized David was gone.

"David!" she screamed. "Da—vid!"

Desperate to protect Isabel, Jessie hunched over the child and prayed for God's mercy as the gusts continued their assault.

Finally, Isabel began to wiggle and squirm, and Jessie realized the winds had calmed and that the roar was fading. She and Isabel had survived. Chills traveled throughout her body as she thanked God for hearing her desperate prayers.

"We're okay," she murmured in the child's ear, then offered sweet kisses of comfort across the top of the toddler's head. "We're okay," she said again for herself.

Too frightened to venture out, she remained huddled beneath the overpass. She knew she'd just lived through a miracle. Without a doubt, God had called her to this exact place to catch Isabel. And as Isabel cried in her arms, Jessie didn't know if she'd ever be able to let go of the child.

Then she heard a truck on the highway overhead and the loud muffler jolted her back to reality. She had to find David. They needed help. When she tried to stand, her cramped legs rebelled.

"Help," she called out. "Help us."

Clutching Isabel, she fought through high weeds and wet grass to reach the crossing highway above. At first, neither her car nor David's were anywhere in sight. Power lines sparked, and somewhere close by she heard the insistent mooing of a frightened cow.

At the top, frustrated that the pickup truck was long gone, she turned slowly, looking in all directions. First, she spotted their cars. Hers, though right-side up, was riding piggyback on David's. But that didn't matter. She had to find David.

"David," she yelled over and over again.

Looking at the highways she marveled that there wasn't another car in sight. She tried her cell phone, but once again she heard the all-circuits-busy signal.

A solitary crow flew overhead, and as she followed its elegant flight across the pasture she thought she saw a speck of red. David had been wearing a red golf shirt. It had to be him.

"David," she called again as she ran toward him. "I'm coming."

Isabel securely clasped her arms around Jessie's neck and molded her body to Jessie's. Halfway across the field, the red dot came into better focus and there was no doubt that she'd found David.

But why didn't he move? Why didn't he at least wave? Surely he'd heard her calling his name.

She stumbled as she tried to move faster than physically possible. Each time she fell to her knees in the rutted and uneven field, she picked herself up and trudged forward. By now, Isabel had spotted her daddy and was calling for him. "Dada, dada, dada."

After a race that seemed to last forever, Jessie fell to her knees beside David. Lying on his back, his hands and legs were spread out from his sides as if he were trying to create a snow angel. With his eyes shut, he looked peaceful and without pain.

Then she saw the slow rise of his chest. She gasped with relief. "David," she said. When he didn't respond, she turned to Isabel. "Dada, dada," she said, encouraging the little girl to chant with her. As she listened to Isabel's sweet voice, Jessie briefly closed her eyes and prayed for guidance. Other than a basic CPR course, she had no emergency training. She knew it wasn't wise to move someone who might have a neck injury, and judging by the distance David had been thrown and the position he'd landed in, his injuries were most likely serious.

He needed a miracle. But hadn't they already had their share tonight? They were too far from the highway for someone to spot them or for her to flag anyone down. And she couldn't leave David alone in the field. Pulling out her cell phone, Jessie tried again to dial for help. She dialed and then pushed redial over and over again, but she couldn't get through to the emergency number. Finally, in desperation, she called her parents' house. The phone rang and rang, until her father finally picked it up. Without wasting a second, she explained what had happened and where she was. He told her to sit tight and that help was on the way.

With Isabel still in her arms, Jessie scooted as close to David's side as she dared and took his hand into hers without moving his arm. His breathing continued to grow deeper, settling into an even rhythm, and his hand felt warm and strong—good signs, she quickly decided.

There was only one thing she knew to do and that was pray.

Oh Lord, she began, *if only there could be an ambulance close by. If David's injuries are serious, every second counts.*

Looking off across the field, Jessie had no idea how widespread the devastation might be. The tornadoes might have touched down only in this little corner of the state, or they could have traveled for miles, destroying all that was in their path. And if that was the case, the emergency vehicles might already be in use or unable to get here.

Studying David's hands, she couldn't help but wonder what kind of man he was. His fingers were long and sturdy and his nails were clipped short. Everything about him, from his dark hair and his smoothly shaved face to his stylish golf shirt and navy Dockers, was neat and trim. He had that dependable businessman look about him. And she'd only had to hear Isabel say "Dada" once to know he was a devoted father.

Looking right at David's fingers, she thought she felt them move. She discounted the light flutter to reflexes, or too much hope on her part. But the second time he rubbed his palm against hers, she was sure. Then Isabel shrieked with glee and clapped her hands. Jessie looked up and directly into David's dark brown eyes.

She'd never in her life seen eyes so beautiful. Never seen a smile so tender or thankful. Dark bangs feathered across his forehead, and without thinking she gently brushed them aside. Pressing the back of her hand against the side of his cheek, she sighed in relief.

No words needed to be spoken. Together, they'd beaten the odds. When David covered her hand with his and their fingers interlocked, Jessie reveled in the comfort.

"Thank you," David said, his voice a notch above a whisper. "Thank you for saving my baby." When he gazed at Isabel, who'd been distracted by a spring flower, his eyes misted over.

Jessie's throat closed off as a wave of emotion crested in her heart. "I was no hero. It's as if God dropped her in my arms. I'm just glad I was able to hold on and protect her." And she hadn't let go of the little girl since.

Goose bumps rose on her arms as she relived the moment again in her mind. "Isabel came through without a scratch," she assured him. "But what about you? Are you in a lot of pain?"

When he tried to sit up, Jessie cautioned him to lie flat. "I called my father, and he should be here any minute now." *Send an ambulance,* she prayed silently. "I don't think you should move until you've been examined by an EMT."

David sighed loudly with a resignation that worried Jessie. Either he was hurt more badly than he appeared, or he was just exhausted. Whatever the case, he seemed unwilling to let go of her hand.

So the three of them sat in the field in the middle of nowhere and waited. When Isabel plucked a brightly colored flower and presented it to David, he smiled.

Yes, Jessie thought, *everything is going to be okay.*

At the sound of an ambulance's siren, Jessie felt a tiny tremor of emotion. As soon as help arrived, their fragile bond would be broken. And that saddened her in a way she hadn't expected. Clutching Isabel with her free arm, she hugged the child tightly and kissed her on the top of her head.

Clearly moved by the tender expression, David squeezed Jessie's hand.

As her father and the EMTs raced toward them, Jessie released David's hand to stand and wave. Looking back down at him, she encouraged him with a smile. They would go back to their separate lives, and while their paths might never cross again, she knew she'd never forget him and Isabel. This brief moment had cracked open a part of her heart she'd thought she'd sealed off forever.

Chapter Two

Lying in the deep, wet grass, David knew he'd forget neither Jessie's kindness, nor her courage. She had protected his daughter as if Isabel were her own, and for that he would always thank God.

Looking up at her, he smiled, and when their eyes met he knew she felt the same measure of relief he did. He couldn't think about what might have happened.

"You're sure Isabel's okay?" he asked again.

"Yes," Jessie said gently. "Though she could use a bath. In fact, we could all use a bath, a hot cup of tea and a change of clothes."

Jessie grinned, and when she did, so did Isabel. David didn't know when he'd seen a more beautiful sight.

The EMTs set down their equipment and immediately went to work on David. While they assessed his condition, monitored his vital signs and checked for spinal injuries, David watched Jessie and Isabel.

A few feet away, Jessie embraced her father, who had just arrived. ''Daddy, I've never been so glad to see you in my life.''

''Me, too, sweetheart. Me, too.''

''Do you know where the storms hit tonight? Was there much damage?'' she asked, eager for information.

''From the radio reports I've heard so far, a series of tornadoes touched down. However, most of them were south of Springfield, and they all hit in less-populated areas like this. So far, no fatalities have been reported, and I'm praying there won't be any. But there has been a lot of wind damage to homes and barns in this area, as well as several power outages across the city.''

As one EMT prepared to transport David to the hospital, the other checked Jessie and Isabel, declaring them both in good condition.

Jessie met David's eyes briefly, and though she didn't say anything, he knew her thoughts. They easily could have been fatalities. But somehow, and for some reason, God had spared them.

Jessie kept pace with the EMTs and her father, as they hurried back across the field to the ambulance. Though her arm tired from holding Isabel, she refused her father's offer of help. Neither did she let go of David's hand. Though the storms were over, she still felt the need to hold on to him and to feel his strength.

When they reached the ambulance, the EMT tried to keep her from riding with David, but she shoved her way into the vehicle and refused to budge. The driver turned on the siren, and in less than fifteen minutes the ambulance pulled up at the emergency room entrance. Greeted by hospital personnel, the ambulance doors opened, and Jessie finally was forced to let go of David's hand.

"Dada, dada," Isabel said, as they wheeled her father away.

"It's going to be okay. Everything is going to be just fine, you'll see," Jessie promised.

Following behind, Jessie reached the lobby area as David's stretcher disappeared down a hallway and behind a thin white curtain.

Having driven his own car to the hospital, Jessie's father, Don, caught up with her from behind, giving his youngest daughter a squeeze on the shoulders.

"Where's Mom?" Jessie asked, suddenly aware of her mother's absence, though feeling her prayers.

"She's staying at your sister's house tonight."

"Is Maria sick again?"

Don nodded. "She's got a cold."

"Just when she seemed to be getting over the worst of her morning sickness. At this rate she's going to be sick her entire pregnancy.'' Though Maria was in her seventh month of pregnancy, she still suffered from bouts of morning sickness. During the past two months, both Jessie and her mother had taken turns helping Maria; because she had been so fatigued, she needed help caring for her eighteen-month-old son and husband.

''Did the storm hit near them?'' Jessie asked.

''Strong winds gave them a few tense moments, but everyone's fine.''

''That's good news.''

A woman wearing white pants and a colorful smock approached them. As she handed a clipboard and pencil to Jessie, she said, ''We'll need your husband's medical and personal history.''

Refusing to take the clipboard, Jessie said, ''Oh, he's not my husband. He's my...'' She stumbled over the words. What was David to her? They really weren't even friends. They were barely acquaintances.

With ease, Don stepped in to explain. ''My daughter just happened to be on the highway at the same time as the young man when the tornado struck. I'm afraid we really don't have the information you need.''

Finally, Jessie found her voice. ''His name is David. David Akers.'' Turning to her father, she added, ''He's Liz and Bart's son.''

''Well, why didn't you say so?'' Don exclaimed.

Then his pleasure quickly turned to concern. "I'm sure I heard the Akers were leaving for an extended anniversary vacation in their motor home."

"Thanks for your help," the hospital employee said, before she returned to the admittance desk.

"What a night," Jessie exclaimed to her father as she wiped her forehead with her sleeve.

"You need to go home, take a shower and crawl into bed."

"I will," she said, "but not until I know David's okay." She'd wait in her wet, grimy clothes all night if she had to. "Besides, I can't abandon Isabel."

Holding out a finger to Isabel, Don waited until she grabbed hold of it, then gently shook her hand. "Good grip," he said, much to the toddler's delight. Opening his arms, he attempted to take the little girl. While Jessie appreciated her father's thoughtfulness, she wasn't ready to release the child. And obviously, Isabel wasn't ready to release *her*.

Staring at Jessie's father, Isabel's eyes teared up, and she threw her arms around Jessie's shoulders and buried her small face in the base of Jessie's neck.

"Looks like you've got yourself a new friend," her father said, shoving his hands into his pockets.

Jessie nodded. "I'm just glad I can be here for her."

"Since it could be a while before we know anything about David's condition, why don't I get us a cup of coffee from the vendor down the hall, and you can tell me the whole story.''

"A cup of coffee sounds great. And while you're doing that, I need to find some dry clothes, diapers and a snack for Isabel.''

Thanks to the help of a nurse, Jessie attended to Isabel's needs. Then, as she'd promised her father, Jessie recounted the past few hours. She told her father everything. *Almost* everything. She didn't tell him how tightly David had held her beneath the overpass. How she'd gathered her strength from his every breath. She didn't tell him how cold her hand had felt when she'd been forced to let go of David's at the hospital. And glancing down the hallway toward his curtained cubicle, she didn't tell her father how desperately she wanted to hear good news.

When Jessie shifted Isabel's weight to her opposite hip and shoulder, she noticed the toddler had dozed off. Lightly patting her back, Jessie realized how exhausted Isabel must be.

"Let me take her for a little bit,'' her father offered again.

Jessie shook her head. "She doesn't know you, and I wouldn't want her to wake up and be frightened. She's been through enough trauma for one night.''

And Jessie had a feeling this little girl had already

experienced more upheaval in her short life than most children ever did.

"I'm fine," she assured her father. Though, if she were to tell the truth, she longed to crawl into her soft bed at home and sleep for hours. Her body ached from head to toe—though the discomfort wasn't from holding Isabel. Her exhaustion was mental. It'd been a long night, and the longer they kept David the more worried she became. If she didn't hear news about David soon...

Finally, she sought out her own answers. While Isabel had been awake, Jessie hadn't ventured back to where David was being treated because she didn't think Isabel should see him surrounded by doctors and medical equipment.

Now, because he'd been moved to a different area, it took Jessie a few minutes to locate him. When she did, she saw that he was hooked up to what she thought was a cardiac monitor, and a doctor and a nurse were talking to him.

With David's head turned away from Jessie, he didn't realize she watched through a narrow opening in the divider. She started to back away, not wanting to interrupt, but then inched forward. It wasn't her intention to eavesdrop; she just wanted to get a better look at the man who'd protected her during the storm. Until now, she'd been running on adrenaline, seeing what was before her, yet not really seeing anything at all. If she'd had to describe David, she would have omitted the intensity of his eyes and the serious curve of his lips. But if anyone had quizzed her on the strength of his embrace or his determination to beat the raging winds, she could have talked at length about his stamina and bravery.

She wasn't sure what gave her away, but David turned toward her. For just an instant their eyes met, and Jessie read the questioning stare as if she'd known him all her life. Turning until she could show him Isabel's sleepy face, she made the okay sign with her thumb and first finger. David smiled and then returned his attention to the doctor.

In the waiting room, Jessie settled into a chair, while her father talked to a woman at the admittance desk.

"I was asking if they'd been able to contact David's parents. Even if they're out for the evening, I'm sure they must have a cellular telephone with them," he said as he sat down beside her.

"What did she say?" Jessie asked, stroking the back of Isabel's head.

"David instructed them not to call his family, nor his late wife's family who lives in Ohio."

"Really? That's odd." The news not only surprised Jessie, but concerned her. However, it really wasn't her place to judge David's decisions.

"I'm sure Liz and Bart would want to know," her father continued. "And I'm sure David could use their help when he gets out of here. Someone's got to look after this sweet one.''

''True. But this is David's call.'' However, until now, Jessie hadn't thought beyond the present. What if David wasn't released from the hospital tonight? Or even if he was, would he be able to take care of his daughter? Jessie pressed her lips against Isabel's forehead. If it were up to her, she'd just take this little girl home and keep her forever. But she had an Internet business to run, and Isabel wasn't her responsibility.

Sensing her father was becoming restless due to his inability to help, she suggested he check in with her mother and Maria.

Don jumped up as if he were pleased to be doing something. Borrowing Jessie's cellular phone, he walked a few steps away to make the call.

As she sat alone in the cushy chair in the corner of the busy hospital waiting room, Jessie hummed under her breath. When Isabel stirred, lifting her head to look at her, Jessie thought her heart would melt. And then it did.

''Mama, mama, mama,'' Isabel said.

Jessie's father was still talking on the telephone when the nurse told Jessie that David had asked for her. Expecting him to be dressed and waiting to be discharged, she was disappointed he still wore a hospital gown. However, it was good to see him sitting up.

Isabel instantly jumped with excitement and leaned toward her daddy's arms. When David didn't raise his hands, Jessie sensed his injuries prevented him from holding his daughter, so she moved closer, allowing father and child to kiss.

"It looks like they're going to keep me overnight. And depending on the test results, I might be here a day or two." She could tell by the way he kept looking at his daughter that he'd never spent a night apart from her and that just the thought of being separated devastated him. "I was really hoping they'd let me go home tonight."

His eyes said what his heart couldn't put into words. He was going to have to find someone to watch Isabel overnight.

"What can I do to help? Can I call your parents?" she asked, as if she didn't know he'd told the admittance nurse not to.

David bit down on his lip.

"Is there a neighbor or another family member, then?"

Before David could respond, she heard a deep voice say, "David Akers? Well, what are you doing here?"

"I'll be," David said, with obvious gladness. "And I could ask the same question, Reverend Peters."

"I'm visiting family and friends," the distinguished-looking man said. "You know you can't pastor a church here for twenty years and not know half the city. One of my dear friends was brought in with kidney stones, and I wanted to check on him." Still focused on David, the reverend had yet to notice Jessie. "Are you okay?" he asked David.

David sighed. "I might have a slight concussion, as well as some internal injuries. They're going to keep me overnight for observation. We had a little run-in with a tornado tonight."

"My goodness, thank God you're okay. And little Isabel, was she hurt?"

At the sound of her name, Isabel started jabbering, and Reverend Peters turned toward Jessie. His shoulders relaxed instantly, and he said, "Well, I'll be, if it isn't Jessica Claybrook." His glance bouncing between David and Jessie, a knowing smile lit his face. "Well, well...I'll be."

Realizing the reverend's thoughts were headed in the wrong direction, Jessie rushed in to explain. "By God's grace, we happened to seek shelter in the same place tonight."

Reverend Peters's smile merely deepened. Patting Isabel on the back, he looked at David as he spoke. "Your little girl couldn't be in better hands than Jessica's."

"Jessie's been an angel tonight," David agreed.

The white curtain parted, and a nurse told Reverend Peters that his friend had been released. "Though I'm sorry for the circumstances, it was good to see you both. God bless you," he said, hugging Jessie and Isabel, then shaking David's hand.

As soon as the reverend disappeared, David said, "I haven't seen him since I was a boy, though my parents have kept in touch through the years."

"What a small world," Jessie marveled. "He married both my sisters."

"We may have more in common than a highway overpass."

Though David grinned, Jessie could tell he was tired, achy and needed his rest. And so did Isabel.

"I hate to impose on you..." David began.

"Just tell me what you need. I want to help." Jessie leaned forward for emphasis.

"Normally, I'd call my parents. But they just left on an extended vacation in their RV, and I don't want them rushing home for me. However, I'm sure one of my sisters will watch Isabel for the night."

"I'd be happy to call them. I don't want you to worry about her. I'll make sure she's taken care of until I reach them. You need to concentrate on getting well."

"No arguments there," David said, lying back on the bed. Jessie wrote down the numbers he quickly rattled off.

Surprised by the telephone prefixes, Jessie hesitated at the curtain opening. "Your sisters live near

St. Louis? Won't it take them at least a couple of hours to get here?'' Taking a deep breath, she made a quick decision. "Look, since it's so late, why don't I spend the night with Isabel? It's the most practical and the easiest solution for both you and her.''

David shook his head. "I can't ask you to do that. You've already gone to too much trouble. You've been here for hours. I'm indebted to your kindness.''

It occurred to Jessie that he might not trust her with his daughter. Isabel was all he had, and, after all, Jessie was a virtual stranger. "I understand you'll be more comfortable if she stays with one of your sisters—''

"No, it isn't that,'' David claimed, and the light in his eyes told her he trusted her. "You don't owe me this. Really, I've got family that will help.''

Jessie pressed her lips against Isabel's forehead, then held the child close enough for David to hug and kiss her good-night. With Isabel's arms anchored tightly around her neck, Jessie couldn't help but say, "Please, let me stay with her tonight. We've all been through enough. She's comfortable with me. It might be best for her.'' *And for me,* Jessie thought.

David stroked his chin between his thumb and fingers. "I really don't want to impose.''

"I want to do this for you. And if the situation were reversed, I know you'd do the same for me.''

Somehow she sensed that about him. That he was the kind of man who'd help someone in need.

David opened his mouth to speak, but before he could say no, she said, "Then, it's settled. I'll stay with Isabel for the night."

The orderly arrived to take David to a higher floor for more tests. As he wheeled him away, David said, "I'll call you later."

"Don't worry about us. We'll be just fine."

How could she not be? She was holding in her arms the one thing she wanted most in the world.

Chapter Three

"It looks like we are a family. At least for to-night," Jessie said as she stored the personal items she'd picked up at her home in her father's car and headed to David's house. Her father, who'd taken a cab home, had arranged for her car and David's to be towed to the garage, and a nurse had loaned her a car seat for Isabel.

"We're doing great," she said to the sleeping toddler. "We're doing just fine. This is going to be a piece of cake."

Then she hit a pothole she hadn't seen in the dark, and the unexpected jolt woke Isabel, whose pout quickly escalated into a full-blown cry.

Jessie tried to soothe the child with songs and soft-spoken promises, but nothing quieted her. And then Jessie made the big mistake—she told Isabel that before she knew it, her Daddy would be home from the hospital. The mention of David's name upped Isabel's cries by yet another decibel and started her begging for her "Dada."

Unnerved by the desperate sobs, Jessie made two wrong turns before she pulled into David's driveway. As she parked the car in the garage, she momentarily rested her forehead against the steering wheel and wondered if she'd agreed to more than she could handle.

Her prayer was quick and to the point. *Lord, please help me comfort this child. If I can survive a tornado, surely I can survive Isabel's bedtime.*

As soon as Jessie carried Isabel through the doorway, the child stopped crying. It was almost as if she knew she was home, and just for a second, Jessie felt the same peaceful familiarity.

But that was silly, she thought. She'd never been in David's home before. She had her own home, less than a half-mile away, that she loved.

Having no time to waste on trivial thoughts, Jessie went straight to the kitchen, where she prepared a small bottle of milk for Isabel, just as she'd seen her sister Maria fix on many nights for her nephew. In the nursery, the milk quieted Isabel, and the child slipped off to sleep as Jessie gently rocked her.

When she was certain Isabel slept soundly, she placed the child in the crib. *Please, Lord, keep Isabel safe through the night.*

Leaving the nursery door slightly ajar, Jessie shuffled down the hallway. With everything under control, she took a quick shower. After changing into a nightshirt, she collapsed on the living room sofa and, too tired to find a bed, instantly fell asleep.

Less than a half-hour later, Isabel's cries woke her. Too softhearted to let the toddler cry herself to sleep, Jessie took her from the crib and cradled her in her arms. Entering the nearest bedroom, which she assumed was David's, she and Isabel crawled into the king-size bed and cuddled beneath the comforter.

As Isabel slowly calmed down, Jessie loosened her embrace and allowed her own thoughts to roam. Inching down the bed, she rolled onto her side so she could study Isabel in the moonlight. She pressed the toddler's tiny hand against her own, marveling at the beauty of her delicate fingers. As she listened to the child's peaceful inhale and exhale, she decided she'd never heard anything so magical.

Swallowing hard, Jessie prevented the old dream from surfacing. She would never give birth to a child of her own. She would never know a moment like this. So in the silent house, she decided to accept this special gift.

When the telephone rang, she almost didn't answer it. But then it occurred to her that her parents or David might need to contact her.

"Hello," David said. "I know it's late—"

Though the telephone had awakened Isabel, she didn't cry. "I'm glad you called. Isabel and I are lying in bed," she said. Then, thinking he might prefer his daughter to be in her own bed, she quickly added, "But if you would like, I'll put her back in the crib."

"If she's happy where she's at, leave her. I hate to admit it but I've spoiled my girl. She loves napping in my bed."

Jessie felt the heat of her blush and was thankful David couldn't see her. Lying in his bed while talking to him on the telephone suddenly seemed intimate. She shook the thoughts from her head and instead asked him how he was doing.

He sighed. "I hope to come home tomorrow. I tried to tell the doctors there's nothing wrong with me. I'm just a little sore."

Sensing he'd told her all he wanted to, Jessie didn't press him for more specific answers. Having just met, he didn't owe her a detailed diagnosis.

Isabel reached for the telephone with both hands, and Jessie said, "I think your daughter would like to speak to you."

"Please, put her on."

His loving tone warmed Jessie. Placing the telephone against Isabel's ear, she smiled, as Isabel jabbered and slobbered over the mouthpiece. Lowering her head, Jessie shared the telephone with Isabel, listening as David sang a familiar lullaby to his daughter.

"She's sound asleep," Jessie whispered, as he started a new verse.

"That's a relief," David said.

Jessie silently agreed, unwilling to let David know she found temporary motherhood a little more taxing than she'd anticipated. Taking care of her eighteen-month-old nephew for a few hours at a time while he napped or played was a totally different experience from being in charge of a child's needs around the clock. The magnitude of the responsibility she'd taken on had begun to sink in.

"If you feel up to it, maybe you could tell me about Isabel's morning routine," Jessie suggested.

"She generally wakes up around seven, and she'll need to be fed and changed. And you'll want to give her a bath and brush her teeth. You'll find her play clothes in the third drawer of the dresser, diapers in the closet, and she likes hot cereal with bananas and milk for breakfast. But I should warn you, she wears as much oatmeal as she eats."

Feeling overwhelmed, yet determined to conquer the morning routine, Jessie switched on the bedside lamp, grabbed a pen and paper and began scribbling notes.

"Just give her a sponge bath in the morning. There's a small plastic tub and sponge on the bottom shelf of the changing table."

"I can give her a bath," Jessie insisted, lest David think he'd made a mistake trusting his daughter's care to her. Besides, how difficult could it be to give a toddler a bath?

"Elaine will be there at nine, so as soon as she arrives—"

"Elaine?"

"Elaine Marshall. Isabel's nanny. I'm sorry, in all the confusion I didn't realize I never mentioned her. She's been out of town visiting her sister. She lives in an apartment over the garage."

Of course, Isabel had a nanny. Jessie had seen the stairway in the attached garage earlier in the evening, but she hadn't given it any thought. It also explained why David hadn't been eager to ask either his sisters or his parents for help.

"Well, that's great. As soon as Elaine gets here, I'll leave for the hospital."

David paused. "Listen, Jessie, I don't want to sound ungrateful, but there's no reason for you to come to the hospital. You've already gone beyond the call of duty. And believe me, you can't know how much I appreciate your help. You give the words *Good Samaritan* a whole new meaning."

Though she thought the comparison was exaggerated, Jessie appreciated David's sentiment. "I have to come to the hospital, anyway," she said. Then she explained about the borrowed car seat and that her father had arranged to have both of their cars towed to a local garage.

"I'm so amazed at how a disaster can bring out the best in people."

"Yeah," Jessie echoed. "If a person didn't believe God watched out for them, a night like tonight certainly would change their mind."

When David lapsed into silence, Jessie swallowed hard. For some reason, in those few seconds, she felt his pain and confusion. Instinctively, she knew losing his wife had challenged his faith in ways she'd never experienced. She wanted to say something meaningful, to assure him that even in the most difficult times, God would never desert him. And she should know.

But before she could come up with an encouraging response, David said, "The nurse just came in. Do you have any more questions about tomorrow morning?"

"No," Jessie said. "Don't worry about your daughter. Get a good night's rest and concentrate on getting well."

"Thanks to you, I feel like I can do that."

"Good night," Jessie said. As she held the receiver tightly, she realized she didn't want the conversation to end. She wanted to know more about this man who'd risked his life to save his daughter's.

"Good night," David said. Then, with a surge of

energy, he added, "Jessie's blue bunny was in the car..."

"Don't worry, I'm sure my father will collect your belongings from the car."

"And Jessie," David added, "tonight was a miracle." And he hung up.

Reluctant to break the connection, Jessie listened to the silence until the telephone company's automatic recording came on the line.

She closed her eyes, but sleep eluded her. Now that she was certain David and Isabel were both settled, she could let herself think about the tornado. Over and over, she relived the minutes she'd spent huddled beneath the overpass with David's arms anchoring her in the tremendous wind. She recalled the deafening *chug,* the sting of gravel on her skin and the way she'd gasped for breath in the damp, swirling air.

And while time would eventually polish the rough edges off these memories, she knew one instant would always remain sharp and clear—the moment David had let go. She would never forget his piercing scream, nor the way she'd instinctively reached for Isabel. Her body trembled with fear at what could have been.

Snuggling next to Isabel, she believed without a doubt she'd been in the right place at the right time. God had dropped this child into her arms.

Thank you, Lord, for this miracle, Jessie prayed, and then closed her eyes and slept.

An early riser, Jessie eased from the bed at 6:00 a.m. Isabel had slept without waking, and she showed no sign of stirring soon.

Uncertain whether she should leave Isabel in the bed alone, Jessie retrieved her laptop from the living room and settled into an overstuffed chair in the corner of the master bedroom. Angling the screen so the glare wouldn't disturb Isabel, Jessie maintained a clear view of the child. She placed a pillow over the computer to muffle the initial modem sounds. Once online, she went immediately to giftsoflove.com.

This was *her* baby.

Three years ago, she'd started the Internet bridal gift registry with a modest inheritance left to her by Grandmother Angie. Though her parents had urged her to buy mutual funds, Jessie had decided to risk it all on a business of her own. She'd had no doubts her grandmother, an adventurous woman herself, would have approved.

In the beginning, Gifts of Love had been an uphill struggle. Instead of staying in the larger metropolitan area of Dallas-Ft. Worth where she'd lived after graduating from college, she'd decided to move back to her hometown of Springfield, Missouri. But after working around the clock, six days a week, she could finally declare giftsoflove.com a success.

As the homepage loaded, Jessie felt a familiar surge of adrenaline. Impressed by the new pages that the evening shift had designed and uploaded, she noted only a few areas that needed fine-tuning.

When she finally glanced up at the clock, over an hour had passed. Shutting down her laptop, she hurried to get dressed before Isabel awoke. She even considered calling David to tell him the night had gone smoothly. Chances were, he was awake. Everyone knew no one ever got quality sleep in a hospital.

She picked up the receiver, then, feeling foolish, set it back down. After staring at the telephone for another minute, she quickly punched in the hospital number before she could change her mind.

"Hello," David answered, sounding wide awake, much to Jessie's relief.

"I thought you might like to know your baby slept through the night."

"That's good. I was worried she wouldn't be able to settle down."

"And how did you sleep?" Jessie asked as she fingered the telephone cord. Not until she spoke did she realize how eager she'd been to hear his voice and to know he'd improved.

"Fairly well. However, I feel like…" In the background, she heard the shuffle of sheets as David shifted his weight on the bed, his discomfort great enough to interrupt his words. "...a dump truck ran over me."

Though Jessie didn't say anything, she assumed David would be out of commission for longer than he might be willing to admit.

"Oh," she said, "Isabel's waking up." Moving to the bed, she held the receiver next to the sleepy child's ear. As soon as Isabel heard her father's voice, she smiled and stretched. Jessie shared the little girl's satisfaction and decided to treasure these special moments God had given her.

Jessie was prepared for the look of surprise when she walked into David's hospital room later that morning with Isabel balanced on her hip.

"Hi, Pumpkin," David called out to his smiling daughter, while his eyes asked why Isabel wasn't at home with Elaine.

When David inched to one side and patted the bed, Jessie securely positioned Isabel between her father's chest and arm. However, she remained close to the bed, just in case the toddler started to squirm.

"Elaine's been delayed, hasn't she?"

As Jessie explained that Elaine's sister had fallen that morning and Elaine was taking care of her sibling's twins, empathy shone from David's brown eyes. "You made the right decision in telling her to stay," he assured her. "I would have told her to stay in Kansas, too."

He kept shaking his head. "I can't believe this is happening to Elaine's sister. She's had a rough time lately." Looking directly at Jessie, he added, "Sometimes, I really have to wonder what God is thinking."

Jessie merely shrugged and offered a tight smile. This wasn't the moment to volunteer her personal insights about God's timing.

Shifting his gaze to Isabel, David relaxed a little. "The bright side is that I get to see my little girl. I wasn't certain you could bring her to my room."

Jessie's smile widened and she touched her fingertips to her lips. "I'm not certain whether it's allowed, either. We just walked in like we belonged here."

"With you in charge, there's nothing to worry about."

Briefly, she met his gaze, surprised by how much his respect meant to her. However, she wasn't about to spoil her image and confess that his neat brick home looked like a disaster zone. By the time Jessie had cleaned up the dining room and kitchen floors, Isabel had dumped the box of toys in the living room, plus she'd knocked over a potted fern and rubbed dirt into the carpet. And while she'd talked to Elaine on the cordless telephone, Isabel had followed her curiosity into the nursery, grabbing at anything within reach. Jessie had stayed one step behind the crawling toddler, but it still amazed her how much chaos Isabel had created before she scooped her up.

"The doctor is going to make me stay another night."

David grasped her hand, forcing her to meet his gaze again. This time she knew what he was going to say before he even opened his mouth.

"You've done so much already. Don't even think about offering to watch Isabel today."

"I don't have to think about it," Jessie assured him. "In fact, I insist on staying with Isabel. We're a team now. You can't separate us. Besides, it's only for one more night."

Chapter Four

Was he letting stubborn pride dictate what was best for his daughter? David wondered the next morning as he hung up after talking to his married sisters.

No, he knew he was right.

In the past year, his parents had devoted a significant amount of their time and energy to helping him and Isabel settle in Springfield. While they had done so out of love, and while he'd admitted to his family that he couldn't have made it without their support, he'd also made it clear that it was time for him to stand on his own two feet. Though it would be so easy to cave in, he knew in his heart it was best for everyone if he took full responsibility for his daughter.

Next, he called the main offices of Hot & Fresh

and made sure the business day was off to a smooth start. As the owner of five Springfield deli and coffee shops, which specialized in thick sandwiches, the best bagels in town and the freshest coffee in the state, he lived a fast-paced life. He was used to solving problems, to anticipating market trends and to outsmarting his competition. He rarely came home until he was too tired to think about anything except his little girl.

But here in the hospital, he hadn't been as successful in fighting off unwanted memories. Though it'd been a little over a year since his wife, Kate, had died after a Florida freeway accident, it sometimes seemed like yesterday. Surprisingly, it wasn't what he saw in the corridors, but what he heard and smelled when he closed his eyes—the pungent medicinal odors mixed with the sweet fragrance of stargazer lilies, the soft shuffle of footsteps punctuated by the constant *ding* of elevator bells, and the hissing, beeping sounds of medical monitors—that summoned the vivid images of the last days of his wife's life.

Now, restless and confined by the square room, David sought a change of scenery. Putting both feet on the floor, he tested his balance and was pleased with the progress he'd made in such a short time. After getting dressed, he slowly headed down the carpeted hallway to the waiting room near the elevators. Despite some interior decorator's fine effort, the scenic mountain mural, the ficus trees and the upholstered furniture didn't fool anyone—it was still a hospital waiting room.

Standing in the bright sunshine, he cautiously stretched his arms over his head. He didn't care what the doctors said, the only thing wrong with him was a few sore muscles. There was no need for him to spend another night here.

He continued to stretch, leaning forward at the waist, then to the side, the back, and the opposite side. When the nearby elevator dinged and the door opened, he looked up and saw Jessie and Isabel.

"You must be feeling better," Jessie said, her smile conveying relief and enthusiasm as she allowed Isabel to kiss her father's cheek.

"Much better. In fact, I'm ready to check out."

"Is that your diagnosis or the doctor's, Mr. Akers?" she asked with a smile that told him not to bother answering.

Determined to prove his point, he opened his arms to Isabel, who immediately leaned into his embrace. And even though his chest muscles tightened uncomfortably with her extra weight, he beamed with pride. It would only be a day or two at the most before he was back to normal.

"Now what do you think?" he asked. But before Jessie could answer, the elevator stopped on the floor and her parents stepped off.

"Mom, Dad." Jessie greeted her parents with a

quick kiss on the cheek. "I didn't expect to see you here this morning."

"We were running errands and decided to check on David. If there's anything we can do to help, don't hesitate to ask."

With Isabel anchored on his left hip, David extended his right hand in greeting as he said thank you to Don and Helene.

"Mom and Dad speak often of you," he said.

"We think the world of them." Helene smiled as she spoke and playfully squeezed Isabel's hand. "And the way your mother's always talking about Isabel, I feel like I know this little one." Seeking David's gaze, Helene added, "We're serious about our offer. With your parents out of town, please don't think twice about asking us for help. That's what friends are for."

David nodded with sincere appreciation.

Helene pulled a terry-cloth stuffed rattle from her purse and waved the bright-colored toy in front of Isabel. Instantly, the toddler reached for it, and when she did, Helene took the child into her arms, just as David imagined she did with her own grandchildren.

David was surprised when the Claybrooks made themselves comfortable on the institutional sofa. They obviously intended to stay for a while. But one glance at Jessie and his astonishment dissolved. The Claybrooks bequeathed kindness and compassion in the same way most families passed on blue eyes and curly red hair. And because they were friends of his parents, they were willing to lend him a hand.

Drawn to the healing warmth of the sunshine, David shuffled closer to the floor-to-ceiling windows. Holding his body erect, he watched children on swings in the playground below. "I thought I'd have heard something from the doctor by now."

"Hospitals operate on their own timetables. Try to relax," Helene said. Then, turning toward Jessie, she added with a teasing lilt, "I'm guessing that as in your case, patience isn't one of David's virtues."

"Really?" Jessie said, though her smile gave her away. "I would never have guessed that."

"Hey," David said, "I'm the injured party here. How about a little sympathy?"

Again Helene addressed Jessie. "Like he doesn't think we know he's heading straight to the office as soon as he's released from here." She turned back to David, softening her voice. "Your mother tells me you push yourself too hard. I know she'd want you to take a few days off. I promise you, the business won't collapse if you take a short vacation."

David smiled, just as he did when his own mother launched into this too-familiar argument. Before he could respond, Helene added, "I've been saying the same thing to Jessie for the past three years. A little time off doesn't hurt anyone. It helps you put your priorities in perspective."

Curious as to Jessie's reaction, David met her

gaze. Where he'd expected to see a stroke of irritation or a touch of defensiveness, he saw shades of pain. He didn't know what had happened in her past that compelled her to work long hours, but whatever it was, the spidery roots of disappointment and heartache ran deep into her heart.

David swallowed hard, suddenly realizing how little he knew about Jessie. What did she do for a living? Did she work until she was too exhausted to do anything at night but fall into bed? And if she prayed to God, what did she ask for?

When she turned her head, as if she were uncomfortable with David's scrutiny, he continued to study her profile. He had learned a few things about her in the short time they'd known each other. She had courage and heart, a smile that cheered him and the instincts of a mother. And looking at her strong cheekbones, feathery blond hair and expressive green eyes, he couldn't deny her beauty.

But despite all this, he couldn't let her continue to watch Isabel. His daughter was his responsibility, and he'd imposed on Jessie's kindness far too long. He didn't care what she insisted.

Signaling to Jessie and the Claybrooks that he'd be right back, David walked back to his room. He silently sighed when no one seemed intent on following him, but were more interested in entertaining Isabel. And when Helene distracted his daughter with a "horsey ride" on her knees, the childish giggles following him down the hallway, he knew it would be quite a while before Isabel missed him.

Though Jessie couldn't decipher all the emotions she'd seen cross David's face, she believed his abrupt departure had to do with her. When he glanced at his daughter, his intent became clear.

She wasn't sure why—whether it was pride, distrust, or that David simply found it difficult to ask for help—but she knew he was determined to hire a baby-sitter.

Jessie stood in the doorway and listened as David punched out several telephone numbers in a row, with the same result. Each person he talked to was either on their way out of town, already had plans or had a cold.

David shoved the telephone receiver into its cradle, then stared out the window.

"No luck?" Jessie said, making her presence known. He obviously had a pool of backup baby-sitters he frequently called upon.

Startled by her voice, David jumped. "No," he admitted, though he kept on staring out the window as if the answer to his dilemma were merely a puzzle he had to solve.

"Looks like you're stuck with me for one more day," she said.

"I really appreciate your offer, but as I've explained, you've already done too much." Immedi-

ately, David punched out another number, but when
no one answered he continued to hold the receiver,
pushing the disconnect button with his thumb. He
wasn't going to give up easily.

"I don't know why you're being so stubborn."
The truth was, she didn't know why *she* was being
so insistent or why it suddenly seemed so important
to her. Rationally, she could think of a dozen reasons why she should be helping David locate a sitter.
But her heart kept reminding her of how perfectly
Isabel fit in her arms, how satisfying it was to feel
chubby hands grasp her neck and how invigorating
she found the child's fresh powdery scent. "I guess
you just have a hard time accepting help."

"Yeah, I guess I do." David sounded grumpier
by the moment.

"If you can't find anyone else, I assume you'll
have to call your parents or sisters." Though he
hadn't elaborated, she assumed he would go to great
lengths not to call upon his family. And she understood that. After she'd moved back to Springfield,
her parents had tried to take her under their protective wing. It was only natural. And there'd been
times when it would have been so easy to call them
for help—when the washing machine had flooded
the house or when she'd sprained her wrist or when
her car had broken down in a busy intersection.
However, she'd been determined to take care of herself, and in the long run she'd been right. With every

situation she'd tackled, independence had grown a little easier.

"Calling my parents isn't an option." He spoke sharply, and then apologized. "Of course, they'd take Isabel in a heartbeat. And that's the problem. I won't ask them to do that. In the past year, I've relied on them far too much. When I first moved back to town, I couldn't have made it without them. But it's time I started standing on my own two feet."

"Then, I guess that leaves me. It's just one night." Which was exactly what she'd said when he'd been admitted to the emergency room the previous day.

Though his frown irritated her, she respected his determination to take care of his daughter without his family's assistance.

David replaced the receiver. "I suggest you catch your breath, then, because as you know, a few hours with Isabel can wear out the fittest woman."

When Jessie laughed, David did, too. They relaxed in the conspiratorial moment.

"Are you going to take a few vacation days?"

Turning the tables on her, David said, "What would you do?"

Before she could respond, her cellular telephone rang. Raising her eyebrows, she conceded his point, and answered the call from her office.

"Let me get back to you," she said, quickly ending the call and turning her cellular phone off. Meeting David's gaze, she said, "Do you mind if I use your phone? I forgot I wasn't supposed to have my cell phone on in the hospital."

David nodded, and she dialed her office.

She efficiently defused the problem at work, then went over telephone and fax messages, as well as the mail she'd received that day. Positive nothing urgent needed to be handled, she told her assistant she'd check in with her later in the afternoon.

The bemused light in David's eyes provoked her into a smart remark. "You made your point earlier. Like you, my family thinks I spend way too much time at the office."

"But what do you think?" David asked, as if he genuinely cared.

"I think I'm lucky to have a company and a work environment I love, and I don't take it for granted."

But what she wouldn't admit was that as much as she thrived at Gifts of Love, her company didn't begin to fill the emptiness inside her heart. Gifts of Love couldn't give her the love and companionship she longed for. And most importantly, it couldn't give her the one thing she wanted most in the world—a child of her own.

"You must have a pretty flexible schedule or an understanding employer, to be able to take off work in order to watch my child," David said. "Please, don't tell me you're using vacation time to do this."

"I have a great boss. The best, if I do say so."

His puzzled look said he believed this was a clue he should have understood.

"I own the company," she explained.

"Really?"

He'd weighted the word with curiosity and admiration, instead of the disbelief she so often heard.

"Gifts of Love. We're an Internet bridal registry company."

"Then, that explains why I haven't heard of it," David quickly added.

Though the message was subtle, Jessie received it loud and clear. David Akers wasn't looking for a bride. And that suited Jessie just fine. She'd had her heart broken one too many times, and marriage definitely wasn't in her near future, either. However, her reluctance to fall in love did complicate her desire to have children. For the time being, she'd resigned herself to believing God might not make all her dreams come true.

As if he felt the same awkwardness she did, he pushed the conversation forward. "What exactly do you do?"

Thankful to have the subject shifted to safer territory, Jessie launched into a description of Gifts of Love. Though she spoke with pride, she wasn't egotistical. Hard work, a few lucky breaks and a lot of prayer had held her company together during its tenuous beginning.

"So basically, we build a personalized Web page for each engaged couple. From the site, family and friends can review the gifts the couple have registered for and place online orders, as well as send e-mails, post photographs, and even set up a family chat room."

David folded his arms over his chest, his dark eyes intrigued by the business scenario. "But how do you make money?"

Jessie understood he wasn't being nosy or prying into her personal finances. He was genuinely interested in the concept of her business.

"Through advertising. Plus, we negotiate incentives and percentages with the department and specialty stores we're linked to, based on the sales we generate."

Nodding his head, he added, "In other words, you can link your customers to any business that ships. Amazing."

"Exactly," Jessie said, feeling the same excitement she'd felt the day she incorporated. "I originally thought we'd appeal most to people who have a significant number of out-of-town wedding guests, but people who live across town from the wedding couple use our service just as much."

"Wow," David said. "I'd like to hear more about what you do, but I'm afraid if we don't rejoin your family, they're going to come looking for us."

"I'd like to hear more about what you do, too."

While she spoke the truth, what she'd really like to hear more about was the man.

"I still owe you that free cup of coffee next time you're in the deli."

She started to say, *That's a date,* but stopped herself just short of embarrassment. "I'm going to take you up on that."

As soon as Isabel saw David, she started to whine and reach for him. When he didn't move fast enough to satisfy her, little tears fell down her cheeks and she wiped them away with pudgy fingers. Once David settled on the sofa, Helene gently set Isabel on his lap, and all was right with the little girl's world again.

"Your daughter thought you'd gotten lost," Helene said as she glanced from David to Jessie.

Jessie blushed, eager to explain their absence. "I needed to ask David a question, and then I got a call from the office. I shouldn't have had my cellular on in the first place." The faster she spoke, the guiltier she felt. But she couldn't help it. Her parents gazed at her with that familiar he's-an-eligible-bachelor look.

She was thankful when a delivery boy stepped off the elevator and attentions turned elsewhere. "I've got an order for Don Claybrook."

"What a thoughtful idea," David exclaimed, as he tore open a bag with the Hot & Fresh deli logo and began passing out sandwiches and bags of chips to everyone.

Jessie's dad winked. "We thought some good food might make the wait more bearable."

Though she was hungry, Jessie suddenly felt compelled to escape the cozy atmosphere. The last thing she needed was for her family to get serious matchmaking ideas.

Picking up Isabel, she said, "I think this little girl needs to go home, eat her lunch and take a nice long nap."

As Jessie reached for the diaper bag, Isabel's blue bunny and the keys to the rental car her father had secured for her, Helene said, "Won't you at least eat something first?"

"I think I'd better get Isabel home." How could anyone argue with that?

"Well, at least take a sandwich with you," her mother insisted. "Can Daddy and I help you? Do you want us to stop by later?"

Within seconds, Jessie had more offers of help than she needed. "Thank you all. I'm going to settle Isabel in, and call the office. I've got my laptop with me, so while she naps, I can get some work done."

"That's exactly my point."

Jessie didn't miss the message in her mother's fretful eyes. Her mother was certain Jessie was taking on too much, stretching herself too thin.

"I don't mind, Mother, really," Jessie insisted

boldly. For a moment, mother and daughter stared at each other as they silently rehashed old issues.

As much as Jessie loved living close to her parents, she did tire of her mother's worries. Helene didn't like the long hours Jessie worked, nor the frequent business trips. And she'd been upset recently when Jessie had turned down several dates that she and her friends orchestrated. "How are you ever going to get married if you don't go on a date?" she'd asked.

"If it's meant to be, it'll happen when the time is right," Jessie had responded.

But she did understand that some things in life simply weren't meant to be. Not everyone got married, raised a family and then lived happily ever after.

Behind them, a woman wearing a long white coat cleared her throat. In unison, they all turned to greet Dr. Fiddler.

"The news is good. The tests all came back fine this morning. They're putting your paperwork through now. You can go home." When David started to stand, Dr. Fiddler said, "Whoa. It'll take a few minutes for them to process everything. In the meantime, I want to go over a few things with you."

Intent on hearing the doctor's instructions, Jessie inched closer to David. Dr. Fiddler stated clearly that David was to take it easy for a few days, and that he was to schedule a follow-up appointment for the end of the week. As if Dr. Fiddler had this young man's number, she said to them, "And we're all going to make sure he doesn't overdo it, aren't we?"

The response was unanimous, and though David pretended to be annoyed by the overprotectiveness, Jessie sensed he truly appreciated the concern.

"In that case, Isabel and I'll wait," Jessie said.

As soon as they finished eating, Jessie's parents said their goodbyes, but not before once again offering to help.

"Your parents' kindness overwhelms me," David said, after the elevator doors closed.

"They're pretty special people," Jessie agreed.

David nodded, his gaze locked on hers. As she inhaled deeply, he unexpectedly reached out and lightly touched the side of her cheek with his fingertips. "It seems to run in the family."

Jessie was searching for the perfect response to the awkward moment, when the nurse interrupted them.

"Everything's set," she said. "If you'll sign these forms, you can be on your way."

David wanted to walk, but he respected hospital policy and allowed the nurse to wheel him to the front door. Carrying Isabel, Jessie hurried ahead to get the car and meet David at the front entrance.

As soon as David buckled his seat belt he said, "Let's go home."

Jessie swallowed hard, then let the same words escape her lips. "Let's go home."

Chapter Five

Though David could have carried the box with flower arrangements and magazines he'd collected during his short stay at the hospital into the house, he knew better than to argue with Jessie when she told him she'd come back for his things. A few feet ahead of her, he slowly climbed the front porch steps of his brick home. Pausing to inhale the fresh air, he enjoyed the view of the neighborhood.

Recent rain and rising temperatures had greened the front lawn. But while the neighbors' flower beds brimmed with colors, his still held winter mulch. Begonias, petunias and marigolds needed to be planted. Trees and shrubs waited to be trimmed and shaped. The yard needed mowing. The list grew daily.

In theory, buying a home had seemed like the best

thing for Isabel. Had he considered his own needs, he would have moved into an efficient condominium where he could have lived amongst other single adults. Not because he was interested in dating. No, he had no plans for matrimony. But simply so he wouldn't have to see happy families every time he backed out of his driveway.

This house was for Isabel. He didn't want her growing up isolated. He wanted her to be surrounded by children her own age, and though he often felt a stab of pain, deep down he believed he'd made the right decision.

Reaching into his pocket for his house keys, he found an empty pocket at the same time he heard Jessie turn the key in the lock. With Isabel's head on her shoulder, Jessie stepped across the threshold then turned to face him.

"Isabel's asleep," she whispered. "I'll put her in her crib."

David nodded, amazed at how peacefully his daughter slept and how naturally she molded her body to Jessie's.

With his gaze focused on Isabel, David didn't see Jessie extend her free hand, the keys to his house dangling from her fingers. Then she jiggled the keys, and he took them. She wouldn't be needing them again.

After Jessie disappeared down the hallway, David wandered around his living room. It felt good to be home where he could listen to his favorite CDs, relax in his recliner and watch his daughter sleep all night long if he so desired.

Lost in thought, he eased into the dark brown leather recliner. Minutes later, he inhaled Jessie's fresh fragrance before he heard her nearly silent footsteps on the carpet.

"Can I get you anything?" she asked.

"Not a thing. I'm just going to sit here and relax."

"Then, I'll let you be. My laptop is in the bedroom, so I'll check in with the office from there. Call me if you need me."

David raised his arm, and if Jessie had been just a half step closer, he would have grasped her hand. "Listen. I'm feeling pretty good. Isabel is sleeping. We'll be fine on our own. Even if Elaine doesn't drive in until tomorrow morning, we'll be okay."

Jessie looked at him with a stare that said he was crazy if he thought he'd get rid of her that easily.

"I'm not leaving. And that's final," she said.

Before he could protest, she left the room. Feeling more exhausted than he wanted to admit, he decided to let the issue go for now. Within minutes, he was sound asleep.

Two hours later, he opened his eyes.

"Jessie," he called out softly. Slowly, the fuzzy vision cleared.

"Well, it's about time you woke up," she said brightly from the doorway.

"Is Isabel still asleep?"

She arched her eyebrows in disbelief. "She slept for forty-five minutes."

"Where is she?"

"She's playing in her crib. Quite happily."

"Then, I suggest we leave her there."

"How about a cup of tea?" Jessie offered.

"Only if you'll make yourself a cup, too."

"Okay, I'm ready for a break," Jessie said, a little surprised he'd asked her to join him.

A few minutes later, Jessie emerged from the kitchen with two cups of tea and a plate of chocolate-chip cookies.

"Peppermint tea," she explained. "Brewed with loose leaves. It's supposed to soothe the stomach, the nerves and whatever else needs calming."

"Good choice," he said. Picking up a cookie, he held it beneath his nose as if he intended to savor the rich aroma forever. "However, it's this beautiful sugar concoction that impresses me most. Elaine is a health food fanatic, and she purges my refrigerator and cupboards regularly."

"Well, I won't tell if you won't." Jessie sipped her tea thoughtfully. "Something I heard my mother say to you at the hospital made me think the deli's a family business."

"It is." David reached for a second cookie.

"When I moved back to Springfield, I bought out a chain of fledgling delis. My father had just retired from the fire department, and my mother was an accountant. Working together seemed like a great decision." Taking a bite of cookie, David chewed slowly. "I don't know what I would have done without their help. The success of the delis is as much theirs as it is mine. How about you? Does any of your family work with you?"

Jessie shook her head. "Not directly. My father's an attorney, and his firm handles company legal matters. My mother has made a career of volunteer work. My middle sister has three children and lives in Texas. And my youngest sister, Maria, lives in town—she's seven months' pregnant with her second child. When I can, I help her out with babysitting and errands."

"That explains your knack with Isabel."

He didn't know why, but the same disillusionment he'd seen in her eyes earlier reappeared.

"I'm not sure I have a knack with children, but I do love kids. Plus, when you're the aunt you can spoil them rotten and then take them home."

Leaning his head against the recliner, David studied Jessie as she lovingly bragged about her nieces and nephews. The sparkle in her eyes and the excited movements of her hands left no doubt she adored her sisters' children. If it were possible, the more she allowed her love to show, the more radiant she became. Her deep-rooted beauty went far beyond her shiny blond hair and lovely eyes.

With their teacups empty and the afternoon slipping by, he knew he should check in at the office and allow Jessie to do the same. Isabel wouldn't play quietly for long, and then there wouldn't be a minute's peace until the toddler fell asleep for the night. But the lilt of Jessie's voice mesmerized him, and instead of excusing himself to use the telephone, he peppered the conversation with enough questions to keep it going.

"I can't believe our paths have never crossed before now," Jessie said.

"It's amazing, isn't it."

"There are some who would say it's God's timing that's kept us strangers until now." Jessie kicked her shoes off, then casually pulled her legs up onto the sofa and sat on her heels.

"Yeah, there's some who would say that." Having grown up less then a mile apart, they'd gone to the same schools, attended the same church and loved the same teenage hangouts. Though he'd known of her family through his parents, being a few years older he'd never noticed Jessie.

"But you don't think so?"

Jessie seemed eager to hear his reply, his answer important for some reason he didn't understand.

"I think it's as simple as our six-year age difference." When she pursed her lips as if she wasn't quite convinced by his argument, he added, "For one brief moment, I do think it was God. We were brought together during a tornado. Who knows what would have happened to Isabel had you not been there. In that, I see purpose. But as to some great plan for the future—who knows?"

He shrugged as if to ask, *Who could possibly know the mind of God?* He certainly didn't, and he never would understand a God that could take a loving wife and mother from her husband and child.

Worried that he'd been too abrupt, he backpedaled. "Please, don't think I'm not grateful for your time. If we hadn't met beneath the overpass, you wouldn't be watching Isabel."

Jessie pulled a small, terry-cloth bear from a crack between the sofa cushions and smoothed its arms and legs as she spoke. "Granted, I'm here because of circumstances." And because of the instant connection she'd felt with Isabel. "But I'm not so egotistical as to think I'm irreplaceable. Today was short notice, but I know you won't have any trouble finding a baby-sitter for the rest of the week, should Elaine be detained."

David chose his words carefully, because he certainly didn't want to give the wrong impression. "While that may be true, I haven't seen my daughter respond to anyone like she's taken to you since..."

David let the words trail. He just couldn't say it. Though his heart was healing and he had moved forward with his life, it seemed like the worst kind of betrayal to compare any woman to Isabel's mother.

When Jessie's fingers closed around his, he didn't resist the touch. He appreciated the comfort more than he could express, and when he looked into her eyes he had the strangest feeling the possibility of more had passed between them. But he wasn't looking to replace his Kate, and he made sure every woman who came close to his daughter knew it.

Jessie released his hand, and when she did, she gave him a graceful exit.

"You have a wonderful daughter, and I'm thrilled to spend time with her. She's like the icing on the cake for me. I've got a wonderful career with no Mr. Right in sight, so marriage and a family are way off in the future. Spending time with Isabel gives me a little taste of what I'd like to have. Yet, a big enough bite to keep me satisfied until it's my time."

David didn't take his eyes off Jessie as she spoke. While her eyes were bright—almost too bright—it was her hands that gave her away. The longer she rattled on, the more she squeezed and rubbed the bear. While he didn't believe she'd lied, her nervousness convinced him there was much more to the story. But it wasn't his place to pry.

"When you do meet Mr. Right and get married, you'll be a wonderful mother." Picking up on her cue, he rephrased her words, wanting her to be certain he understood she had no designs on him.

She nodded and smiled, but when she sighed, he once again felt the sadness he'd seen in her eyes earlier.

"Goodness, look at the time. I told my assistant I'd check in an hour ago. Do you mind?"

"Not at all," he said, as if he didn't find anything odd in her sudden need to end their conversation. "I need to call my office, too. Plus, once Isabel hears our voices, she'll want to join us. So, get as much done between now and then as you can, because once she's tired of playing alone, you won't have a second to yourself."

Jessie laughed, her smile deep in her eyes, banishing any disturbing thoughts. For just a minute, David wished her laughter would ring forever. He loved the way her voice filled the room, making the air heavy with her heart and soul.

Yes, Mr. Right was going to be one lucky man.

What had started out as a nice gesture—to prepare a simple meal—quickly spiraled out of control.

The oven timer buzzed, and Jessie absently pushed the reset button but forgot to check the dinner rolls. With the arms of a slobbering, babbling toddler wrapped around her ankle, she stirred the marinara sauce with one hand and held the telephone with the other. Isabel gave new meaning to the phrase "feeling weighted down."

"Listen, Audrey," Jessie said to her assistant. Laying the spoon on the countertop, she wedged the telephone receiver between her ear and shoulder and reached down to pick up Isabel. "I trust your judgment on this one. If the customer really isn't happy, we should give them their money back or see if there is any way we can make up for the error at their Web site."

When Jessie playfully touched the tip of Isabel's nose, the child licked her lips. A tug on the ear brought a smile. But it wasn't until Jessie made a face at her that Isabel broke out in a loud giggle.

"I'm sorry, could you repeat the last part?" Jessie asked, realizing she hadn't heard a word Audrey had said. This time Jessie listened carefully, eager to finish work and to get back to preparing dinner. "It sounds like you've handled everything. Have a great evening, and I'll talk to you in the morning."

"What time can I expect you?"

"I'm not sure. In fact, I may not be in at all. Either way, I'll keep in touch."

Before Jessie turned around, she knew by the shift in Isabel's pliant body that David had walked into the room. And when the little arms shot up in the air, silently saying, *Hold me, hold me,* she sensed he stood directly behind her.

When he leaned forward to kiss Isabel on the

cheek, his hair brushed against the back of Jessie's neck, and when he grabbed one of Isabel's hands, his daughter leaned in the opposite direction so that when he clutched her second hand, their loose embrace caught Jessie in the middle. For a few seconds, David and Isabel embarked on a variation of hide-and-seek. Isabel pressed her face against Jessie's left shoulder and then her right. Back and forth Isabel scurried, each time believing her father didn't know where she was until she looked up at him.

Behind Jessie, David, too, moved from side to side, enjoying the light moment with his daughter. Lost in laughter, he moved closer and closer to Jessie, until his hands rested on her waist for balance.

Though David and Isabel seemed oblivious to Jessie, Jessie was aware of every inch of David's body. She felt his warm breath on her ears, the deep timbre of his laughter raised goose bumps on her arms and his fingertips sent tremors throughout her body.

Suddenly David stopped. When she heard him sniffing, she turned to face him. "What do I smell?" he asked. "Is something burning?"

"I don't think so. I turned off the burners and the oven." She gasped. "Oh my gosh, the oven. The dinner rolls." She started to hand Isabel to David, then remembered he was still sore and bruised from the accident. So she deposited Isabel on the floor a safe distance from the range, grabbed the pot holders and removed the sheet of charred rolls from the oven.

In an attempt to either hold back a smart remark or keep from laughing, David bit down on his bottom lip.

Donning her best apologetic smile, Jessie said, "Just because I have a knack with children doesn't mean I can cook."

"I always thought it was senseless to have bread with pasta, anyway. Too many carbohydrates."

"I'm so glad you feel that way." Jessie relied on humor to hide any hint of embarrassment. How could she have burned the dinner rolls? She'd been distracted. While she could do a thousand and one things at once at the office, she wasn't quite as practiced on the home front.

After lowering Isabel into her high chair and fastening the safety strap, Jessie carried plates from the kitchen to the table.

"What can I do to help?" David asked.

"Keep your daughter occupied and happy."

"You're sure that's all?"

"Isn't that enough?" Jessie asked as she threw the rolls in the trash and scrubbed the baking sheet.

While Jessie finished setting the table and carrying the food to the table, David made faces, sang silly songs and kept a smile on Isabel's face.

In the kitchen, holding a steaming bowl of bow-tie pasta in her hands, Jessie stood and watched father and daughter interact. The unnoticed minutes revealed a lot about David. He was a hands-on father. By the way Isabel cooed and giggled and shrieked with glee, Jessie knew the child was used to her father's attention. They had their own routine, and for a moment, Jessie longed to be included. David Akers was the kind of father she'd always dreamed her children would have.

But she wasn't going to have children.

"Uh-oh," David said.

"Uh-oh," Isabel repeated.

At first, Jessie didn't realize they were looking at her.

"We have to put a smile on the pretty lady's face," David said.

Pretty lady. Jessie swallowed. It was just a figure of speech. He meant nothing by it.

David made a face and launched into a childhood song about a tugboat, while Isabel banged on the high chair tray with a spoon.

"Well, that wasn't difficult at all," David said to Isabel when Jessie finally smiled.

"If you could see the two of you, you'd laugh, too," Jessie insisted. "I guess some boys never grow up."

David's eyes twinkled. "That's the best thing about having a child. You get to be one again."

"Do I have to cut your pasta up and feed you, too?" What Jessie said as a joke somehow shouted with double meaning. The mere thought of feeding David a forkful of pasta seemed intimate and more pleasing than she'd ever have anticipated.

David stumbled over a reply Jessie never heard, turning his attention to Isabel. When he finally looked up, he said, "Wow, this smells great."

"Thank you." Though she'd prepared a simple meal—and despite that fact that most everything had come from a jar or a package—he still made her feel as if she'd done something special.

David reached for the serving spoon and placed a meatball on Isabel's plate. As he cut it up and added mashed broccoli, he noticed Jessie hadn't filled her plate.

When he met her gaze, she asked, "I wondered if you'd mind if I said grace?"

David cleared his throat, and Jessie suddenly felt awkward and feared she'd sounded self-righteous. Who was she to come into his home and assert her religious practices upon him?

"To be honest, I'm not in the habit of praying before meals."

Honoring his decision, Jessie reached for the serving spoon. She would say a silent prayer thanking God for this food and this day.

David's hand covered hers, stopping her. "That doesn't mean I don't believe in prayer. In fact, praying at mealtime as a child is something I'll never forget. My parents, my sisters and I all holding hands. It's a powerful memory. But with just me and Isabel…'' His voice faltered, and the tightness of his lips betrayed the pain of a man who felt he'd somehow failed his daughter.

Extending his hand, David said, "Maybe she's not too young to appreciate grace. Would you pray?"

Jessie nodded. Clasping David's and Isabel's hands, she said a short but heartfelt prayer. She had so much to be thankful for. She had loving parents, a career she enjoyed and good friends. She had her safety and health. And now, God had wondrously brought David and Isabel into her life.

Jessie said *"Amen,"* yet the three continued to hold hands. Glancing from Isabel to David, Jessie knew for the first time in her life what it would feel like to have a family of her own. Her dream was so close, so real. And then Isabel squirmed, the connection ended and she remembered this was not her family.

"Let's eat," David said.

Jessie smiled brightly, determined not to let her feelings show.

Later that night, Jessie watched David hang up the living room telephone. Unaware of her scrutiny, he rubbed both temples, then, pushing his shoulders back, he cautiously rotated them. Though he continued stretching, it was his eyes that held her attention:

they were darkened by uncertainty and confusion. She knew the talk with Elaine hadn't gone well.

Jessie cleared her throat. "She's going to be gone a few more days."

David nodded, then rubbed the back of his neck again. Moved by compassion, Jessie stepped forward, intending to massage his stiff shoulders, but at the last second she shied away from such an intimate touch.

"So, what did Elaine say?" As if she feared her hands might reach out for David's shoulders, Jessie clasped them at her waist.

David leaned against the wall, his arms crossed over his chest, and sighed. "She doesn't feel right about leaving her sister."

"I don't blame her." Jessie thought of her own sisters and how they'd always supported one another. When she'd had the operation three years ago, they'd been at her side throughout her recovery.

"I understand her dilemma, and I told her to stay in Kansas and that I wouldn't hear of her coming home until she felt confident her sister could manage on her own."

"Did Elaine have any idea how much longer she'd be needed?"

"A few more days, perhaps a week at the most." Glancing at the clock, David said, "It's too late to do anything about this tonight."

"I'm sure everything will work out in the morning."

"Yeah, I'm sure it will," he said softly. "But you don't have to stay here tonight. Isabel and I will be fine. I can take care of my daughter. She'll sleep through the night, and first thing tomorrow I'll line up a temporary nanny."

Jessie bit down on her bottom lip, keeping her thoughts to herself. David sounded overly optimistic for a man who hadn't had any luck securing temporary help during the past two days.

"You're certain?" Jessie gave him a chance to change his mind. She didn't feel good about leaving, yet neither was it appropriate for her to stay if he insisted he could manage on his own.

"Okay, but only if you promise to check in with me in the morning."

"I promise," David said. "And I will find a way to repay your kindness."

"I've already told you, that's not necessary."

She gathered up her things, then tiptoed into Isabel's room and kissed the sleeping child goodbye. Walking out of David's house took more strength than she'd anticipated. As soon as she backed the rental car out of the garage, she paused in front of the redbrick house. Leaving Isabel didn't feel right.

Later...as she entered her own dark house, she shivered, though the thermostat was set at a comfortable temperature. For the first time, her home seemed too quiet, too lonely. She crawled into bed but slept lightly, listening for Isabel to cry out in her sleep.

The next morning, she awoke tired and groggy. Wrapping a fringed cashmere throw around her shoulders, she eased onto the bedroom window seat and prayed silently as the sun began to rise.

My heart feels different. She spoke to the Lord as she would a best friend. *I don't know how to explain it. Something is changing inside of me. Something I don't fully understand.*

For the past three years, she'd dedicated herself to Gifts of Love, shoving aside all thoughts of marriage and family. But as she'd held Isabel during the raging tornado winds, it had been as if she'd cradled her old dreams. In the solitude she found the courage to admit the truth from which she'd tried to hide— her work would never fill the void inside her.

But it will have to be enough, she thought, *because for now, it's all I have.*

As Jessie continued to pray and meditate, her thoughts repeatedly returned to Isabel. Sitting in holy silence, she couldn't shake the compelling feeling that God wanted her to remain in Isabel's life a little longer. The hows and whys, she didn't understand.

Jessie lingered for a while in the warmth of the morning sunlight, and then showered and dressed.

She had every intention of going straight to the office and putting in a long day.

But a mile down the road, she changed her mind and turned left toward David's house. The closer she came to his house, the more slowly she drove. He had said he'd call if he needed her. And he hadn't called. She couldn't just show up on his doorstep, could she?

Still, she couldn't ignore the feeling deep in her heart that Isabel needed her. Jessie pulled over to the side of the road and prayed again. *Am I just acting out of my own need? Have my desires cluttered my ability to hear Your voice clearly, Lord?*

She took a deep breath and followed her heart, having no idea where it would lead her.

Jessie rang the doorbell and then waited and waited. And the longer she waited, the more worried she became. Surely David hadn't taken Isabel anywhere this early.

Finally, she heard the dead bolt slide, and David opened the door.

"You look awful," she said, too astonished to be polite.

"Thank you. I don't feel so good, either."

Despite David's gruffness, the relief in his sleepy eyes told her he was glad to see her. But before he could explain what had happened, Isabel's sobs interrupted them.

"Let me get her," Jessie insisted. Rushing down

the hallway to the nursery, she found the little girl standing in her crib, clutching the railing. Tiny tears flowed down her rosy cheeks, and as soon as Jessie touched her she knew the child had a fever.

"There, there," she said, clutching Isabel's sweaty body against her chest and gently bobbing her in the air. Within seconds, the toddler quieted.

David stood a few feet away, his dark hair ruffled and his shoulders slumped with fatigue.

"She fussed all night, and she seems to feel miserable." David caressed his daughter's forehead. "I called my sister, and she said to give her baby aspirin and as much fluid as she'll take, and to call the doctor if her temperature spiked."

"Precious baby," Jessie murmured to the drowsy child. Then she looked up at David and offered him a smile of encouragement. Raising a child on his own had to be scary.

David sighed loudly, then pushed his fingers through his hair. "Would you mind staying long enough for me to shower and dress?"

She knew it took a lot for David to ask this favor. He wasn't a man who easily admitted he needed help.

Jessie nodded, a tiny piece of God's mosaic becoming clear to her. "Of course I'll stay."

The time flew for Jessie as she rocked the cranky child. Every time Isabel would fall asleep, she'd cough or sneeze, and then Jessie would have to calm her all over again.

Though David looked slightly better after his shower, exhaustion pulled at his facial muscles. One look in his despairing eyes and Jessie knew why she'd felt so strongly about stopping by this morning.

"You're in no shape to do anything," she said, taking charge. "You need to get some rest. You're not going to do anyone any good until you do."

"But…"

When he was too tired to fight her, she knew she was right. "I've got my laptop with me. I can work as effectively from this house as I can from my own office." That wasn't exactly true, but due to the nature of her business she could keep on top of things from here.

"I can't let you—"

"You don't have a choice. You need me." And though she didn't understand why, she knew she needed him and Isabel, too.

"Besides, you thought it was tough getting a nanny when Isabel was well—with her sick it'll be even harder. Most day-care centers won't even take her now."

David sneezed, and for the first time Jessie noticed that his eyes were red and watery and that he, too, sounded slightly congested.

"You're sick, too. You've got to get some rest."

She looked down at the child in her arms. "If this is contagious, I've already been exposed, so I might as well stay. There's no use infecting anyone else."

"Okay," David reluctantly conceded. "But only until I can make more permanent arrangements. And only if you'll let me pay you."

"Fine," Jessie agreed, though she had no intention of accepting his money.

David shuffled out of the room, leaving her with Isabel.

Oh, Lord, she silently cried out, *where do we go from here?*

Chapter Six

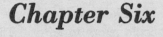

"Jessie, I'm home," David called, the instant he walked through the door.

"Jessie? Isabel?" There wasn't an answer. He hadn't realized his eagerness to share his news until Jessie hadn't greeted him.

One day had flowed into the next, and before he'd known it, Jessie had ended up helping him all week. With both him and Isabel suffering with sinus and bronchial symptoms, he'd had no choice but to accept her assistance. She'd been a godsend—picking up prescriptions, feeding him chicken noodle soup along with plenty of orange juice, and most importantly, rocking Isabel to sleep when he'd been too achy to get out of bed. Fortunately for them all, she'd remained healthy.

Not until he'd seen the dawning smile on her face

the other morning, when he'd felt strong enough for the first time to make the morning coffee, had he understood how spoiled he felt in her presence. Of course, he hadn't been fooled into thinking she appreciated his company as his late wife once had. His and Jessie's easy companionship wasn't like that.

As much as he'd enjoyed Jessie's company, he was still thankful Elaine would be back by morning and that life could return to normal. Though Jessie tried to hide the dark circles under her eyes with extra makeup, he knew temporary motherhood exhausted her more than she admitted. She couldn't continue balancing work with caring for Isabel any longer.

Glancing around the house, David noticed the toys were neatly stored in the toy box that had been his when he was a child, the living area had been dusted and vacuumed and the house smelled of warm apples and cinnamon. It wasn't until he spied the bouquet of fresh flowers on the dining room table and the new peach candle on the kitchen counter that he realized what was really different. For the first time since he'd moved back to Springfield, his house looked lived in.

He heard the garage door motor, then the bang of the door between the garage and kitchen, and finally Jessie's footsteps.

"Is that you, Isabel?" he called.

"Dada, dada, dada," his little girl answered in a healthy voice.

Jessie smiled, her cheeks as reddened by the spring wind and sun as Isabel's were. She handed Isabel to him, removing the toddler's jacket while he held her squirming body.

"If I'd known you were going to be back so quickly, I would have waited—you could have taken Isabel for a ride in her stroller. It's a beautiful day to be outdoors. And to quote my mother, 'Fresh air and sunshine are God's best medicines.'"

Jessie's thoughtfulness went neither unnoticed nor unappreciated. "I didn't think I'd be home this soon, either. I didn't have to wait to see the doctor, and then I wasn't in her office more than fifteen minutes."

"So?" Jessie prompted. "Don't keep me in suspense."

"I got a clean bill of health regarding both the tumble I took during the tornado and the cold. I can resume a normal schedule."

As if she'd never heard better news, she threw her arms around him and said, "This calls for a celebration."

Feeling the excitement in the room, Isabel clapped her hands, as if Jessie and David were playing a fun game.

"We should go out to eat," Jessie suggested.

David raised his brows. "With a toddler?" A

woman like Jessie should dine in restaurants with candles, soft piano music and tables set with white linen, crystal and single-stem roses.

"A hamburger and fries sounds mighty good to me," Jessie said without hesitation. "And then we could come home for dessert."

"I get it," David said, nodding with understanding. "You didn't have time to bake the chicken. That's no problem. I told you before, you don't have to cook dinner. I'm perfectly capable of fixing something to eat. Besides, do I look like a man that's gone hungry in the past year?"

As Jessie's gaze slid from his head to his toes, David suddenly felt self-conscious about the ten pounds he'd put on during the winter months. No more cinnamon rolls with morning coffee, he promised himself.

"You look healthy and happy to me," Jessie finally said. "But now that your appetite's returned, I did promise to cook a special dinner tonight. I can't let you get sick again."

"Don't worry," David said, pressing his finger against her lips to silence the apology. The intimate gesture would have slipped by him unnoticed, if Isabel hadn't copied him by patting her chubby hand against his lips.

Seeking a graceful exit, David playfully grabbed his daughter's hand and pretended to gobble her fingers. Isabel's glee provided the perfect distraction and allowed David to face Jessie again.

"Are we on for dinner?" he asked.

"Give me a minute to freshen up."

"I'll get Isabel ready and meet you in the car."

Ten minutes later, David backed the rental car out of the garage. For a brief moment he thought of his late wife and realized how much he missed being a family. While it wasn't Jessie's fault, old resentments rose up. This was the way his daughter's life should have been.

During her college years, Jessie had eaten her share of cheeseburgers. Still, she'd have testified in court she'd never eaten one as juicy or as scrumptious as this one. And, miracle of miracles, Isabel had somehow managed to confine her mess of pickles, ketchup and hamburger crumbs to a small area directly beneath her high chair.

With a few cold French fries—which she treated more like a toy than a treat—happily occupying Isabel's attention, David leaned back in the booth as if he were in no hurry to leave. Though Jessie had promised her personal assistant she'd read through the file of new contracts, she decided they could wait another hour or so. It'd been too long since she'd had good, adult conversation. Not that she was complaining. She adored Isabel. But she also missed the daily camaraderie she enjoyed at the Gifts of Love office.

Taking a sip of iced tea, David said, "Has this week with Isabel completely scared away any thoughts you might have had about motherhood?"

Jessie smiled as she shook her head, but deep in her heart she felt the old wound bulge with regret and frustration. But it wasn't David's fault. He didn't know what God had denied her. He couldn't possibly know how much this time with Isabel meant to her.

"Are you kidding? Isabel's an angel. It's not every day I get a chance to help someone out like this."

"Still, you must be eager to get back to a regular routine. I know I get grumpy when I'm out of mine for too long."

The direct challenge of his gaze convinced her he needed her to say she couldn't wait to get back to running her business full time.

She sidestepped the question. "I did detect a bit of grumpiness."

A smile simmered on his lips. "Hey, I wasn't that bad, was I?"

"You didn't frighten me."

"Seriously, I'm sure you really won't miss the smelly diapers or the nighttime cries."

Because she didn't see any reason to confess her deepest desires, she appeased him. "Sure, I'm looking forward to getting back to work. But in the meantime, this has been a great break for me. You know, sometimes a person needs to step away from their everyday life in order to appreciate it.''

And she did appreciate Gifts of Love. She appreciated how it attempted to fill the void in her life.

"That's so true." David cleared his throat as if he were about to confess something. "I didn't want to move back to Springfield. But when my father told me about the local chain of delis that was for sale, I had to seriously consider the idea.''

"Because of Isabel?''

"Exactly. Moving back here made it possible for her grandparents, aunts, uncles and cousins to be part of her everyday life. Not to mention all the ways they've helped me.''

"But?" Jessie asked, curious about what motivated David.

"But it wasn't exactly the life I'd thought I'd have.''

Jessie nodded with understanding. She'd always believed a husband and a house full of children were part of her future. But no matter how carefully she'd made her plans, life had taken her in a different direction. Why God would deny her the deepest desire of her heart was a question she struggled with.

"What was your life like before you moved home?" she asked. When uneasiness flickered in his eyes, she regretted reminding him of old hurts. She reached across the table and briefly placed her hand upon his. "Forgive me for asking such a personal question. It's really none of my business."

Yet, she wanted to know more about the life David missed. Somewhere between what he'd given up and the new life he'd created in Springfield was the real David. She wrote her interest off to curiosity. She wanted to know how he'd survived such disappointment and loss without becoming embittered and cynical. She wanted to know because though her loss was different, she had yet to truly deal with it.

"I don't mind," David said. His voice cracked slightly, and he took a sip of tea. His urge to talk seemed as strong as her need to hear his story.

"We lived in Fort Lauderdale, which in itself is a world away from Springfield. The pace is faster, the people are more diverse and there are wonderful cultural opportunities." David paused. "I don't want to imply in any way that Springfield isn't a fine place to live. But our life was in Florida. Kate loved living near the ocean, and she loved working with me. We were a great team. We started the first restaurant, never guessing it'd be successful. We were so happy. If only I'd known it would end so soon." David looked away in an attempt to hide the deepest pain.

For a moment, Jessie let the silence hang between them in honor of a woman she'd only met through the eyes of a fourteen-month-old child. When David finally looked back, she said, "You can't live with what ifs. It's too easy to judge life through the rearview mirror. It's what you do with today and tomorrow that really counts."

David pursed his lips as he gave serious thought to her comment. "Someday when you're a parent, you'll understand that this feeling... I'm not sure how to describe it. It's like I can never do enough for Isabel. Whatever I do, I fall short."

"I think you're being way too hard on yourself," Jessie said.

"Can I be too hard on myself when this little one's future depends on me?" David smiled at his daughter, messing her wispy hair with his hands. "I'm this little girl's mother and father."

"For now," Jessie said softly, fearing she treaded on risky ground. "But in the future..." She swallowed, then started again. "Someday, you'll meet someone, fall in love and get married." Then hastily she added, "Not that anyone could ever replace Isabel's mother."

"You're right. No one can replace Kate. And it's a moot point, because between raising my daughter and managing the delis, I don't have time for a relationship."

Jessie got the message loud and clear. Kate's death had devastated David. And though he seemed fine on the outside, Jessie knew it would be a long time before he'd ever trust in love again.

"Well, someday..." Jessie said. It was the hopeless romantic in her that made her push, just the same. Plus, it was much easier to imagine a happy ending for someone other than herself.

"I'm not interested in a relationship." David's eyes challenged her to disagree one more time.

"Sorry," Jessie said, suddenly fearing he'd misunderstood her romantic notions and thought she might be applying for the position of wife and mother. "It's a hazard of my occupation. I'm so used to working with happy couples that I think everyone ought to find that one soul mate that fulfills them."

David eyes softened just a bit. "Really?"

Jessie cleared her throat, uncomfortable with the way his eyes held her captive. "Really."

"Then, why haven't you found your special guy?"

"What makes you think I haven't?"

When David nearly choked on his iced tea, she guessed he wasn't thrilled with her retort. Then she realized why. Though she hadn't intended to confide in him, she felt forced to correct the ghastly assumption he'd just made.

"I was engaged to a man I met in college. We shared the same Christian beliefs, we had common goals and interests, and we seemed to have a special bond I thought would last a lifetime.''

"I'm sorry. It's just the way you said you'd already met Mr. Right.'' As David apologized, a deepening blush crawled across his cheeks. Folding his arms over his chest, he continued. "I'm a little sensitive in this area. You wouldn't believe how many friends have tried to set me up on dates. Or how many cookies and cakes have been dropped by the house by women who were just in the neighborhood. Or the number of offers I get weekly to baby-sit Isabel.''

"Oh, I'd believe it. You're a successful man with an adorable daughter.'' She stopped herself from adding that he also looked great in faded blue jeans, he knew how to curl a woman's toes with just the hint of a smile and he possessed a self-confidence and purpose in life that inspired awe.

"But I'm not good relationship material,'' David insisted.

"That's what sparks the challenge.''

"In other words, if I were to come across really nice and sensitive and let women know I'm eager to get married, they'd leave me alone?''

The twinkle in David's eyes amused her. "Could be. But then, that course of action could land you and Isabel in some really deep water.''

"Thanks a lot.'' David smiled as he signaled the waitress for the check.

"I never claimed to be an expert in matters of the heart. In fact, if there is one thing I don't understand it's love. And just for the record, I'm no longer looking for Mr. Right. He's going to have to find me."

"And would you know him if he stared you in the face?"

Jessie dared to meet David's gaze. "Of course I would."

As soon as they walked into the house, the telephone rang. "Let the answering machine pick it up," David instructed. "I'm going to give Isabel a bath and put her pajamas on, before I do anything else."

When Jessie hesitated, he insisted, "Whoever it is can wait."

Jessie pursed her lips as if letting a telephone ring unanswered was against her better judgment, then disappeared down the hallway. David assumed she'd gone to pack her things. With Elaine returning tomorrow, he expected Jessie would be eager to go home tonight.

The bath routine had taken David months to streamline, but after a lot of practice he could now bathe his daughter without soaking himself, the carpet and anything else that might be in the way. Tonight, however, was the exception.

When the telephone rang again, he deposited a clean and diapered Isabel in her crib and hurried to the kitchen extension. Seeing Jessie at the dining room table sorting through work files surprised him. As soon as she saw him, she covered her mouth to stifle a laugh. He shrugged as if to say, *Yeah, I got a little wet.*

The telephone rang again, and David snatched the receiver. As soon as he heard the worried tone of Elaine's voice, he knew what she was going to ask.

"I understand. You don't have to explain. Your sister still needs you. Isabel and I will do just fine until you can come home."

"Are you sure? It would mean so much to my sister if I could help her with the twins until she gets her cast removed."

"I'm positive, Elaine. Stay in Kansas as long as you're needed," he assured.

Before he hung up the telephone, he felt the heat of Jessie's gaze.

"Did she say how long she thinks she'll be away?" Concern, as well as curiosity, simmered in Jessie's voice.

"I didn't ask. I doubt she really knows at this point. She wants to stay until her sister's cast is removed, and I've got to assume she'll be away at least another couple of weeks."

"Maybe longer," Jessie added softly.

"I can't say the news is unexpected." David rubbed his jaw. It'd already been one long day, and now when he was ready to kick back and relax, he had to find someone to watch Isabel for the next several weeks.

"I'm sure you'll work something out." Jessie raised her brows as if to say she was sorry.

But the situation wasn't her fault. And he couldn't let her continue to care for Isabel. She'd already done too much for him. She had a business to run, plus family and friends who missed her. Besides, Isabel wasn't her responsibility.

"This doesn't change anything," he said.

Her clear eyes questioned his judgment. "This arrangement is working out fine for me. I can watch Isabel for a few more days. At least let me do that. You can't expect to find someone overnight who'll be available for the rest of the month."

"Jessie, I will not impose on you any longer. I know you're exhausted. You can't keep running your business and watching Isabel. They're both full-time jobs. You're going to burn out."

When her eyes clouded over, hiding her true feelings, he could only assume she didn't want to tell him she was eager for him to find a replacement. But that wouldn't hurt his feelings. He hadn't expected her to help out this long.

Jessie bit down on her lip and turned her attention back to the work at hand. Her cellular telephone rang, and within seconds she was immersed in her own world.

He recognized the intensity and passion he saw

in her eyes because he felt the same zest whenever he persevered through a challenge or celebrated a success at work. It wasn't just the soft silky hair or luminous green eyes that made her so lovely. It was her heart.

She never had said why her engagement ended, but any man who'd let her get away had to be a fool.

Chapter Seven

Jessie began to pray the next morning. *Why did you bring me here? Was it just to remind me of what I might never have? Or do you have another purpose? It seems David and Isabel need me.*

She yawned, moaned and then pulled the covers over her face. It had been after midnight before she finished reviewing the stack of contracts and notes her assistant had faxed. Then she'd tossed and turned for several hours before falling into a fitful sleep.

Her head told her she should pack up her clothes and computer and go home. But her heart had other ideas. Her heart wanted to stay just a little longer.

She mulled over her options. She'd only intended to help out for a few days. She had a thriving business that required her time, energy and leadership.

She couldn't keep playing mommy forever. Yet, in the grand scheme of her life, what would it hurt to work part-time for one more week? Thanks to her personal assistant, the telephone and a computer modem, she could stay on top of any crisis at Gifts of Love.

The safe thing to do was to walk away from this house. To go back to the life she'd created in Springfield. Ever since she'd been here at David's, she'd neglected her parents and her sister's family, her friends, as well as spending too little time at the office.

When she heard the first sounds of Isabel stirring over the baby monitor, Jessie knew what she would do. She didn't wait for God's answer, because she had her own plans.

Jessie nervously listened as the garage door lowered later that afternoon, followed by the slam of the car door and David's footsteps down the hallway to the kitchen, where he grabbed a cold drink from the refrigerator.

Playing quietly with Isabel on a quilt on the living room floor, Jessie pretended it was just an ordinary afternoon and that she hadn't been counting the minutes until David returned from the office. Hiding her eagerness, she didn't even look up at David until Isabel spotted her father and demanded his attention.

Reaching down as they exchanged greetings, David picked up Isabel, kissed her and tossed her gently in the air. She laughed with the innocence of a child who lived in a safe, secure world.

Rising from the floor, Jessie eased out of the room to check in at Gifts of Love. As she passed Isabel, the toddler reached out with one hand and grabbed Jessie's hair. Touched by the gesture, Jessie kissed Isabel on the nose before retreating to the dining room table where she'd set up her temporary office.

Judging by the low volume of Isabel's squeals, Jessie knew David and his daughter were playing in the nursery. But even with them out of sight, Jessie had a hard time settling down to work. It would take time for David to notice all that she'd done, she told herself. She merely had to be patient.

Finally, Jessie blocked out Isabel's happy jabbering and immersed herself in work. After checking in with her assistant, she logged on to the Gifts of Love Web page to view the latest uploads. Out of the corner of her eye, a blur of forest green caught her attention.

When she looked up from the computer screen, David moved quietly toward the kitchen. He pretended to lock his mouth, as if to say, *I'll be quiet. I won't disturb you.*

But just the sight of the dark-haired man shattered her concentration. She listened as he rummaged through the refrigerator and secretly smiled at his sigh of pleasure, knowing he'd discovered the fresh-baked chocolate chip cookies on the counter. He still hadn't put it all together. However, she had confidence that before the evening was over he'd notice all she'd done.

But would her efforts really make a difference? This morning, she'd been certain she'd found the perfect way to convince him she should be the one to watch Isabel. Now, she wasn't so confident.

Jessie tried to corral her thoughts. The sooner she finished her work, the sooner she could relax. The promise of a few minutes with a good book, maybe even a long hot bath and an extra hour of sleep, lured her back to her task.

But only for a minute.

Until David popped around the corner.

In one hand he held a plate of sandwiches and cookies, and in the other a huge glass of cold milk. A wide chalky mustache framed his mouth, and she glimpsed the playful boy he must have been.

"What?" he said, looking instantly to his left and then to his right, as if he couldn't believe he'd done anything to solicit her amusement.

Jessie shook her head, wondering if she should clue him in. Enticing him with the hint of a grin, she waited until his gaze settled on her face, then she slowly licked her upper lip.

For an instant, neither one breathed. Then David swallowed hard, his Adam's apple straining against his taut neck muscles. A kaleidoscope of emotions spun through his dark eyes, and she felt his loneliness, his desire to rebuild his life and his frustration at not being able to trust in love.

Overcome by the intense vulnerability, Jessie looked away. She'd seen more than she should have seen. More than she knew how to handle. Instinctively, she said nothing and allowed the moment to pass. Just because David had been willing to trust her with his child didn't mean he wanted her to know the private longings of his heart.

And though she felt great compassion for him, she didn't want to see his wounds. She didn't want to be drawn close enough to his heart to feel the pulse of his hurt and pain. That would complicate their arrangement and, in the end, keep her from doing what she felt God had called her here to do. To watch over Isabel.

Setting the plate on the table, David regained his composure and wiped the milk mustache from his face. As if the past few minutes had never happened, he pointed to the computer screen and asked, "Is that Gifts of Love?"

Jessie nodded, thankful for the timely diversion. "Would you like a tour?"

"Yeah, I'd love to see it." He glanced down the hallway. "But let me peek in on Isabel first. I left her playing in the crib."

Having assured himself that his daughter could entertain herself, David stood behind Jessie as she pointed and clicked her way through the Internet site.

"That's amazing," David said, seemingly impressed by the graphics and user-friendly layout.

"What a great idea to include baby showers, birthdays and house warmings."

"While I'd like to take credit for the ideas, the expansion seemed so logical it sort of happened on its own. Weddings and bridal showers led to gifts for first-year anniversaries, which then led to baby showers. Once someone uses our service, we're our own best advertisement. Our format is flexible. We can help anyone who's throwing a party or hosting a reception."

"You love what you do," David said with respect.

"I've got the best of both worlds. I'm challenged creatively and intellectually by the business, and at the same time I get to help people celebrate the happy occasions in their lives."

"I hadn't thought of it that way." David stepped to one side to look at her instead of the computer screen.

"People don't celebrate enough. We get so caught up in the big events that we overlook the smaller victories and successes. Those are moments with family and friends we can never recapture."

Leaning against the edge of the dining room table,

his knees inches from where her hands typed on the keyboard, he asked, "What is it that you celebrate?"

She didn't dare say the first thought that came to mind, that she celebrated the days spent with Isabel. The ordinary hours of feeding, bathing and playing with the toddler. The minutes she held Isabel in her arms and rocked her to sleep.

Being with Isabel was a miracle he wouldn't understand—unless she told him she'd never be able to have a child of her own. And there was no reason for her to confide in him. No reason for their lives to become any more entangled than they already were.

"What do I celebrate?" she repeated, stalling for time. "I celebrate..." She hesitated, dipping her chin low enough to break eye contact. "You'll think I'm silly."

"I'm really interested," he assured her. Still leaning against the table, he grabbed the edge with his hands while bending forward at the waist.

Mesmerized by his attentive eyes, Jessie didn't notice how greatly the distance between them had narrowed, nor that he'd commanded her total focus.

"It's hard to think of a specific example." She poked through her recent memory for a piece of her life that didn't seem too personal to share. "We're about to sign a contract that will align Gifts of Love with a very prestigious department store." Jessie paused to show two sets of crossed fingers. "But since we have no control over whether this deal will actually go through, we celebrate the little victories. For instance, when I set the first appointment with the department store executives...after we made our proposal to them...when they told us they were very interested.''

David nodded. ''What do you do to celebrate?''

''Sometimes I let employees go home early. Sometimes I take everyone for coffee or an ice cream. Sometimes we all just let loose with a big office cheer.''

''It's an intriguing way to keep office morale high.''

Jessie backed up, offended by his comment. ''It's more than an office strategy,'' she insisted. ''This is the way I live my life. Life is filled with too many disappointments. Too many things don't turn out the way we want them to. If we only waited to share the huge moments with friends or family or to thank God, life would be dreary.

''But when I find goodness and joy in the little things in daily life, it helps me to keep my life in perspective. I really believe in that old saying, Life's not a destination, it's a journey.''

David rubbed the back of his head, then took a few steps away from the desk and crossed his arms over his chest. ''When I suggested your philosophy is a good morale booster I didn't intend it as a personal criticism.''

Jessie continued staring at him, not quite satisfied with his answer.

David wiped his hand across his mouth and then added, "I guess I just don't find too much to celebrate these days."

Jessie shook her head. "That's really too bad, because you have so much."

"Maybe I'm just more cynical than you are. Maybe I've lost more than you have."

He'd gone too far. No, she hadn't experienced the death of a spouse. But she had losses. She had hurts and disappointments that ran deep. She knew what it was like to be angry with God and question His ways and wonder how on earth you were ever going to live with the path He'd set you on.

Jessie stood so quickly she knocked the chair over. "You don't know what I've lost."

She pushed past him, intent on escaping the house and his dark, probing eyes. But as she grabbed her purse, he rushed up behind her and clasped her wrist.

When she turned to look at him, his intense gaze ignited chaos in her heart. The longer she looked into his eyes, the harder it became to remember why she'd been angry. When he opened his mouth as if to speak, she couldn't help but look at his lips. For one brief second, she wanted to kiss him.

"I'm sorry, Jessie," he said. He spoke softly and with regret. "I can be a real jerk at times."

"I'd say this was one of those times." Afraid her eyes might betray her emotions, Jessie lowered her gaze.

With his fingertips, David raised her chin, forcing her to look directly at him. "I'm really sorry."

"It's no big deal," she assured him. "It was just a misunderstanding."

When he still held on to her wrist, she added, "Really. Everything is fine."

"Okay," he said, letting go, but remaining close as if he didn't know what to do or say next. Then a twinkle appeared in his eyes. "Maybe we should celebrate."

"Celebrate?" she questioned. "What do we have to celebrate?"

"We just survived our first misunderstanding."

While Jessie smiled, deep down she felt odd. Getting past a misunderstanding or an argument seemed too personal, too intimate. Yet she couldn't turn down the inviting gleam in David's eyes.

"And how do you propose we celebrate?"

"We could get a baby-sitter and go out for a nice dinner."

"Tonight?"

"Oh, I'm sorry," David said. "You've got work to do. What am I thinking?"

He'd given her an out, and she knew she should take it. Becoming friends with David would only complicate her life. In a day or so, she'd be walking out that front door and never coming back. But she ignored all rational thought and listened to her heart.

"I didn't know you'd be able to get a baby-sitter on such short notice."

"It's a whole lot easier to get a baby-sitter for an evening than it is to find a temporary nanny."

Jessie pushed her tongue against the inside of her lip, weighing her options one last time. "Tonight it is."

"Perfect," he said.

Perfect. The word echoed in Jessie's mind. What would a *perfect* night with David be like? For certain, she'd need to start with the *perfect* dress, shoes and accessories. And she didn't have anything suitable here.

"I'll need to go by my house," she said. "What time should I meet you at the restaurant?"

"I'll pick you up in two hours," he said.

Jessie nodded, knowing she'd have to rush to be ready that quickly. She scribbled her home address and telephone number on a piece of paper and stuck it under a magnet on the refrigerator, next to David's household to-do list.

She grabbed her purse, then detoured down the hallway to peek in Isabel's room before she left. With her back to the doorway, Isabel lay in her crib, playing with her blue bunny. Not wanting to disturb the peaceful scene, Jessie blew the toddler a kiss and whispered, "I'll be back soon."

* * *

The doorbell rang, and Jessie glanced in the mirror and frowned. The dark slacks and the short, fitted black suede jacket with the long red scarf that had seemed like the perfect outfit ten minutes ago, no longer seemed right. She lowered the zipper an inch, she raised the zipper an inch, but it didn't make her feel more confident.

Rushing down the hallway, she flipped light switches off and grabbed her keys from the ceramic dish on the entryway table. A few steps from the front door, she stopped abruptly. Through the frosted glass panes, she studied David. Standing tall in a tweed jacket, he shifted his weight from one foot to the other, and rubbed his freshly shaved face as if the repetitive action calmed his nerves.

David rang the doorbell again.

Jessie took a very deep breath and greeted him.

"Hello," she said.

"Hello," he echoed.

She suddenly felt as if she were on an awkward first date.

"This is a beautiful house," David said, breaking the silence.

"Thanks. It's taken time, but I'm finally getting everything the way I like it."

"Your flower beds are quite impressive. Don't tell me you're a master gardener."

"Oh, no," Jessie said. "But I've found someone

who is. Though I did work with the landscaping company on the design of the yard. The house came with newly laid sod and a few shrubs, but that was it.''

''I may need to get the number of the company you use.''

''It's yours,'' Jessie said. However in her mind, she heard the words, *I'm yours.* Wow, she thought, where did that come from?

When David leaned his head to one side, Jessie realized he was as curious about the inside of her house as the outside. Caught off guard by his interest, she said, ''How rude of me. Would you like to come in for a moment? Since I haven't been home, the cupboards and refrigerator are frighteningly bare. There isn't even a chip or cracker in the house to offer you.''

David stepped into the high-ceilinged entryway, turning slowly to admire the soft white walls, beige carpet and crown moldings. ''Your artwork really brings this place to life,'' he said as he walked toward an original oil painting.

The comment pleased Jessie. She'd purposely kept the colors and textures of her home neutral and simple to balance the beauty of her burgeoning art collection.

''Do you have a favorite artist?'' she asked. What she'd actually wanted to ask was if he appreciated art or if he'd ever studied art. But to ask that straight out might sound condescending.

"Let's just say, I know what I like," David said. He moved closer to the painting, inspecting the mountain landscape she loved. "Besides, when you have a toddler, there's not much point in investing in anything you have to insure."

The grin that widened Jessie's mouth didn't reach her heart. From the entryway, she could see into the dining and living rooms, and what rooms she couldn't physically see she traveled to in her mind. This was the home of a woman who never expected to have children.

"When did you start collecting?" David wandered ahead of her and stopped in front of a bronze sculpture of interlocking crosses.

"Several years ago. I started with landscapes. I've always loved mountain and ocean scenes. Then I met a Christian artist whose work I loved, and it started me in a whole new direction. My religious art collection is modest, but growing."

She met his gaze briefly and wondered if he sensed she wasn't telling the whole truth. She had started collecting exactly three years ago. Not long after she'd been released from the hospital, and right after her ex-fiancé had betrayed her trust and shattered her dreams for a future filled with children.

Jessie crossed her arms over her chest and shivered. It didn't matter how much she tried to fill the void—whether with art or her business—nothing ever totally eclipsed the ache in her heart that only a child could fill. But for now, God had given her little choice in the matter.

"You may not have many pieces, but I really like what you've selected."

"Thank you." Jessie nervously pulled on her necklace and realized it wasn't fastened securely. When she fumbled with the clasp, David stepped up behind her.

"Let me help."

Her fingers briefly brushed his as she placed the gold chain in his hands. Pushing her blond hair off her shoulders, David easily worked the clasp.

"There," he said, smoothing her hair back into place. With his hands gently anchored on her shoulders, he turned her to face him. "If I haven't already told you, you look lovely."

Uneasy with the compliment, Jessie blushed.

They lingered a little longer, and then David extended his elbow and said, "I don't know about you, but I'm starving. Shall we leave for the restaurant?"

Jessie nodded, placing her hand on his strong arm. Suddenly, she was very hungry. But not for steak and potatoes. She wanted conversation, midnight strolls and warm embraces.

She wanted trouble.

Whether because of nerves or because she was spending too much time with a certain toddler, Jessie rattled on over dinner about her sisters, her business and her art collection, as well as a myriad of other interests. With another woman, David might have found the constant chatter irritating, even boring. But there was nothing mundane about the sparkle in Jessie's spirited green eyes or the charming warmth of her lazy smile. She was beautiful, articulate and intelligent, and she had his full attention.

What on earth had possessed him to suggest they go out for the evening?

He knew better than this. He knew how one kind gesture could be misinterpreted and blown out of proportion. And he couldn't afford to offend Jessie. Not as long as she watched Isabel. He hated being beholden to her generosity, but right now, he didn't have any other choice. He'd yet to secure a temporary nanny. The day-care centers that had come highly recommended had waiting lists. And he refused to ask his family for yet another favor.

Common sense told him it wasn't wise to date the nanny.

But Jessie wasn't exactly a nanny and this certainly wasn't a date. It was merely a thank-you dinner, he assured himself. A way of saying thank you for taking good care of his baby.

The waiter poured two glasses of sparkling water, and Jessie suggested a toast.

David raised his glass and tapped hers.

''To tornadoes, little girls named Isabel and God's mysterious ways,'' Jessie said.

Two out of three isn't bad, David thought, keeping his cynical views to himself. At the moment, he wasn't too keen on God's ways, mysterious or not.

''I wish there was some way I could properly thank you for taking care of Isabel.''

Jessie shook her head. ''How many times do I have to tell you, I want to watch Isabel. Just until Elaine returns. I don't see any point in bringing someone new in for a few weeks, when we've been such a good team.'' A worried look bridged Jessie's eyes. ''I am doing a good job, aren't I? I haven't done anything to—''

Before she could finish her sentence, David placed his hand on hers. ''Absolutely no complaints from me or Miss Isabel. In fact...'' He let the words trail off as he quickly reconsidered sharing his concerns with Jessie.

''In fact?'' Jessie prompted.

Realizing she wouldn't be satisfied until he'd finished his sentence, he said, ''She's pretty attached to you.''

Jessie nodded with understanding, then waved her hand as if to signal that it wasn't any big deal. ''She'll be so glad to see Elaine when she comes back, she won't even miss me.''

''Oh, I'm sure she'll miss you,'' David said, suddenly aware he might miss Jessie even more. But for all the wrong reasons, he quickly told himself. She kept the house neat, she baked wonderful cookies and she made Isabel smile. She made his house feel like a home. For the first time since his wife's death, he'd actually looked forward to coming home tonight.

"So have you found a replacement?" Jessie asked. Hope burned dimly in the back of her eyes.

"No, but I haven't given up. I've got a couple more calls to make tomorrow."

"Have you ever heard the old saying—If it isn't broke, don't fix it?"

David studied her as she sipped her water, looking for some clue he'd missed. "Are you real or are you an angel?"

Jessie wiped her mouth with the napkin. With amusement dancing in her eyes, she said, "I don't recall anyone ever calling me an angel."

"You're certain you weren't spinning around in the eye of the tornado and landed in Springfield by accident?"

"Ouch. You think I'm an accident? That's not a very graceful image."

"Seriously, Jessie. Why are you here? Why is watching Isabel so important to you? I know it's not the money I offered to pay."

Jessie shook her head. "My answers obviously don't satisfy you."

Though Jessie boldly looked him in the eye, he still knew she wasn't telling the entire truth.

"I don't mean to sound ungrateful. You're a kind-hearted woman. Still, you've gone above and beyond common kindness." David leaned forward, intent on reading the discreet emotions in her eyes. Instead, the delicate scent of her perfume derailed his plans.

"I'll try to explain this one more time."

When she leaned forward, closing the gap between them, he felt the tension in her body. She was hiding something.

"There are times in your life when you know you have to do something. You don't understand why. You just know from the bottom of your soul it's the right thing to do. That somehow doing this one thing will change your life forever. And if you miss this chance…" Jessie shivered.

As far-fetched and vague as her explanation seemed, David sensed it was the most honest thing she'd revealed all night.

"I need to watch Isabel." She spoke softly, but with a conviction anchored in solid rock. "Let me do this for her."

David could have sworn he heard her add beneath her breath, *Let me do this for me, too.*

"You know it's easy to put money in an offering plate every Sunday morning," she continued. "But I think God expects more of us than to just tithe our money. I believe he wants us to give of our time and talents in the same way."

After a long silence, David agreed. "Okay. It's settled. I think it'd be best if you watched Isabel until Elaine returns. There's no use upsetting her schedule any more than it already has been. She's thriving with your care, and that's what counts."

Though Jessie nodded and smiled, sadness pierced her eyes. He desperately wished he could understand what drove her to this kindness. It was almost as if she were trying to make up for something she'd done. As if she'd made a bargain with God, and watching Isabel was the prize. But what could she possibly gain from such a deal? He just hadn't asked the right questions.

There was one thing of which David was confident. Whatever Jessie was after, it wasn't him. If he'd thought for a moment that she'd been looking to become a permanent fixture in his life, he would have shooed her out the front door before she ever set foot in his house.

Eager to regain the mood of the evening, David said, "Do you want to know the real reason I changed my mind?"

Confusion narrowed Jessie's eyes. "No," she said hesitantly.

David smiled. "It was the to-do list."

"The to-do list?" Jessie played dumb.

"Yeah, you know that long list of yard work and

household chores that's been hanging on the refrigerator.''

"Oh, you mean that list that doubles daily but never shrinks? At least, not since I've been around.''

"That's the list. You don't know how relieved I am to have the slate wiped clean.''

"It was nothing,'' Jessie said, suddenly turning shy.

"And to get everything done in one day. How did you manage that?''

Slowly raising her eyes to meet David's, she said, "When I set my mind to something, there's no stopping me.''

"I can see that. But really, how did you get the yard raked and mowed, the begonias planted and the front door hinge fixed...?'' He rattled off a long list of tasks he'd put off for weeks.

Though he hadn't noticed a thing when he'd first come home, he'd sensed something was different. Still, it hadn't been until after Jessie left for her home and he'd gone out to get the mail that he'd spotted the bright red begonias. The brilliant blooms had opened his eyes. A few minutes later, he'd noticed the door hinge had been fixed. Thinking it was all too good to be true, he'd run around to the backyard and checked the leaky hose faucet. Not a drop of water in sight. Still, not totally convinced this good fortune wasn't a dream, he'd stepped into the garage. Boxes were stacked neatly, tools were hanging on the wall pegs and the floor had been swept clean.

"Getting everything done in a day was a cinch." Pleasure oozed from her playful smile.

"And what's your secret? I've been trying to get those things done for months."

Jessie leaned forward with a grin that suggested she was about to divulge classified information. "I'm a woman," she whispered.

The fact that he'd been trying to deny all night, now stared him in the face. From her green eyes to her alluring smile to her soft touch, Jessie Claybrook was all female.

David shook the traitorous thoughts from his mind. "So?"

"Listen carefully—" Jessie leaned even closer. As she enunciated carefully, David felt a warm rush with each syllable.

"—I delegate. I don't try to do everything myself."

"That's your secret?"

Lost in the teasing exchange, David leaned even closer, until their foreheads touched. "Your secret's safe with me," he promised.

When she exhaled, he inhaled her breath. And in that moment, he felt something shift within his soul. He couldn't put his finger on it. He only knew that for the first time in too long he felt alive. He felt full of hope.

And her smile scared him to death.

Chapter Eight

"No, Mom, I haven't taken on more than I can handle. I'm keeping on top of things at the office," Jessie said a few days later. Fingering the telephone cord, she struggled to hold on to her patience.

"I just don't see how there's enough hours in your day for this arrangement to work."

Taking a deep breath, Jessie patiently attempted to explain her schedule. "If David needs to be at the deli, then I watch Isabel. Sometimes, he even takes her to work with him. He's got a play area set up in his office. She loves being with him. And when I need to be at the office, he watches her. Actually, I haven't had to cut my hours by that much, and surprisingly this has forced me to be more productive with my time." But the juggling and irregular hours did exhaust her. *That* she wasn't going to admit.

"It seems to me—"

"I understand your concerns," Jessie interrupted. "But there's nothing for you and Daddy to worry about. I'm going to help David out for the next few weeks, and as soon as Elaine returns, I'll be back to my old routine."

"If it's really that simple, why do you have to spend the night there?"

"Mom, please don't read any more into this. It's easier for me. That's why. This way I only have to worry about being at two places in one day instead of three. Plus, David often goes in to work at the crack of dawn. If I'm staying in the nanny's apartment, I can get an extra hour or two of sleep before Isabel wakes up."

"If you say so," Helene said.

"How's Maria?" Jessie asked, changing the subject.

"Except for some swelling in her feet and fatigue, your sister's doing fine."

"I need to call her."

"Well, it looks like you've got your hands full."

Jessie closed her eyes and slowly counted to ten. She'd called her mother to ask whether she thought Isabel was old enough to learn to drink from a cup. What should have been a simple question had given Helene an opening to express her qualms.

"Don't you think that's something David should decide?" she'd asked.

"Well, yes. But I was reading in a book that said by thirteen months children should be able to..."

But Jessie couldn't fault her mother. She understood where her worry came from, and she felt all the more loved for it.

"I'm not too busy to call my sister," Jessie insisted. The truth was, she had taken on more than she could handle. Between work and Isabel, there wasn't room for much else in her life. She hadn't been to church, nor had she talked to any of her close friends in days. But she didn't mind. This arrangement wouldn't last forever, and she aimed to enjoy every minute with Isabel.

By the time Jessie shut down the computer later that afternoon—convinced the Gifts of Love Web site once again ran smoothly—silence had claimed the house. Stretching her hands over her head, she released the tension of the day.

Isabel had been cranky and moody for most of the afternoon, demanding all Jessie's attention. Only when held did the little girl seem happy. Eventually, Jessie gave up trying to straighten the house. By the time David walked in, her nerves were frazzled and the house, like herself, looked like a disaster zone. Dishes were stacked in the sink, dirty laundry overflowed from the laundry room into the hallway and the beds remained unmade. Without a word, she handed his daughter over, eager to escape the domestic chaos for a more organized world—only to learn that technical difficulties had caused the Gifts of Love Web site to go down.

Jessie continued to slowly stretch, allowing the frustration and disappointment to ease from her limbs. Overall, it hadn't been a great day, and she wasn't particularly proud of the way she'd handed Isabel over to her father. Maybe she wasn't mother material, after all.

Listening to the silence of the house, she heard soft music and followed the relaxing jazz riffs to the living room. David was fast asleep in his recliner with a Bible open facedown on his lap. A floor lamp, turned down low, cast an ethereal light upon the room.

Mesmerized by the rise and fall of David's chest, curiosity compelled her to study him. With his mouth open slightly and his eyes closed, he seemed vulnerable, even fragile. But Jessie knew him to be anything but weak. Beneath his strong, muscled body beat the heart of a man who plowed through life with purpose and direction, unwilling to allow heartache to defeat him.

Though she didn't know him well, she admired him. For his daughter's sake, he'd moved back to Springfield and turned a floundering deli and coffee shop chain into a success. That didn't happen with a snap of the finger. That kind of accomplishment required vision, determination and unrelenting perseverance. It required leadership and risk-taking. It required David.

And yet, when he walked through the door at night, no matter how tired or distracted, he became both father and mother to a little girl who thrived on his love.

The businessman side of David intrigued and impressed Jessie, but the father side of him touched her heart. Every time she watched him vanquish Isabel's tears with a hug, every time she heard him sing a lullaby slightly off-key, every time she smelled burnt toast, she felt as if she'd peered through a thick curtain to spy on the real David Akers.

Debating whether to wake him up, Jessie finally decided he looked too comfortable to disturb. Carefully, she removed the Bible and set it on the coffee table, then covered him with an afghan. She wondered what had prompted David to read scripture. He hadn't kept his distrust of God a secret. Could he be experiencing a change of heart?

Folding her arms, Jessie inhaled deeply. She didn't want to admit it, but she found David's life way too interesting for her own good. Whatever he worked out with God—as well as how he raised his daughter—was his own business.

Jessie was only passing through their lives.

She picked up the baby monitor and headed for the nanny's apartment above the garage. At the doorway, she turned to look back. David shifted in the recliner, his eyelids fluttering. For a second, she thought he might awaken and find her staring at him.

It would be so easy, she thought suddenly, to fall in love with a man like David. He was all the things she wanted in a husband and in a father to her children.

Jessie swallowed. She knew better than to wallow in sentimentality. Hadn't she learned her lesson by now? Hadn't her own fiancé—the man she'd loved deeply—betrayed her when he learned the truth about her? She had no reason to believe David or any other man wouldn't do the same, given a chance.

Praying silently, Jessie said, *Lord, help me not to forget that You brought me into this house to care for Isabel. Don't let me get carried away with my own fantasies.*

Too restless to sleep, Jessie woke before sunrise and silently shuffled to the kitchen from the garage apartment. After brewing a pot of strong coffee, she wandered from room to room sipping the hot liquid. As she often did in her own home, she puttered— she fluffed the sofa pillows, straightened a picture, moved a ceramic figurine from a higher shelf to a lower shelf and stuffed a dusty, faded arrangement of silk flowers into a closet. Standing back, she let her gaze slowly travel across the living room, satisfied with the subtle changes.

Home. With each day she stayed, David's home felt more and more like her own. The thought of returning to her always tidy, serene house caused her to grimace.

Jessie knew one way to eradicate the self-pitying thoughts before they conquered her mind—baking. There was something about the bread process—mixing, kneading, rising—that somehow soothed her troubled mind and helped her gain perspective.

Detouring by the nanny's apartment, she exchanged her fleece robe for a yellow T-shirt and jeans, then went directly to the kitchen. Pulling out a selection of David's cookbooks—which, judging by their pristine condition, were seldom used—she went to work.

After narrowing her choices to a half-dozen bread recipes, including everything from English muffins to chocolate croissants to rosemary focaccia bread, Jessie pulled the necessary ingredients and mixing bowls from the cupboards and started to work on a loaf of cinnamon bread.

Humming along with a popular Christian music CD, she mixed and kneaded the warm, elastic dough. Finding the push-and-pull rhythm soothing, she continued past the buzz of the timer.

Oh, Lord, she began, praying with the rocking motion. *Help me to see the big picture. Help me to see where my life is headed, and if I've strayed off track, guide me back to You.*

Overcome with emotion, Jessie's eyes dampened. Was it so wrong to want it all—a career and family? Compared to finding her one true love, building a successful business had been easy.

"Hey, what's got you up before dawn?" Standing in the doorway, David wore a cotton shirt and sweatpants. With his brown hair messy and his eyes droopy with sleep, he appeared as huggable as a treasured teddy bear.

Jessie quickly pressed the back of her flour-covered hands against her eyes to wipe away any stray tears, before meeting his gaze. "Bread," she said, as if he should know exactly what she meant.

He raised his eyebrows.

"I'm baking bread," she repeated.

David stepped into the kitchen and poured himself a cup of coffee. "I can see that. What I want to know is why you're baking bread at this hour of the morning?"

"There's no better time," she said, ignoring his probing gaze. "I've got a busy day ahead. As soon as Isabel wakes up, I thought I'd feed and dress her, and then I need to spend a couple of hours at the office." She paused. "I'm assuming that since it's your day off, you won't need me to watch her."

"You bet. Isabel and I have big plans," David said. Then, unwilling to be sidetracked from the subject of Jessie's kitchen mission, he said, "So you do this often—bake bread in the middle of the night?"

"It's not the middle of the night. And yes, I often...bake bread first thing in the morning." She'd started to say she often baked or cooked whenever her worries prevented her from sleeping. But then he'd ask her what worried her, and she couldn't look him in the eyes and lie. She couldn't tell him the thought of turning Isabel over to Elaine's care made her sad. She couldn't tell him how much she would miss waiting for him to come home, sitting down to dinner together and tucking Isabel into bed each night. They were all simple things. But when you knew they might never be a part of your own life, you cherished the moments you had, even if they were moments that belonged to someone else.

David peered over her shoulder to look at the cookbook, then poked his finger into the springy dough.

"Hey," she said softly. "Are your hands clean?"

"Just washed them," he said as he grinned. "I'm checking out the product."

"I was doing fine before you came along." She shaped the kneaded dough into a ball and placed it into a greased bowl.

"What are you doing?" David moved closer to inspect her work.

"You're kidding, right?" Jessie couldn't decide

if he was putting her on or if he really didn't know the fine art of baking bread.

David's smile slid from his face. "Seriously, why are you putting the dough back into the bowl?"

"You really don't know?" She found his ignorance on the subject amusing.

"No, I don't know, and when I'm big enough to admit I don't know something, I don't appreciate being laughed at."

She didn't think she'd offended him, but then, she didn't know him well enough to tell if a twinkle lurked behind his somber brown eyes.

Thinking of the sleeping toddler, Jessie glanced toward the baby monitor that she'd set on top of the refrigerator. All remained quiet in the nursery.

"It's the irony that's making me laugh."

"Care to explain?" David hopped up on a nearby stool and sipped his coffee.

"As the owner of a successful chain of deli and coffee shops which specialize in fresh-baked breads and pastries, I'd think you'd know a few baker's secrets."

Continuing to work, Jessie lightly greased the top of the heavy ball of dough, covered it with a thin cotton dish towel and placed it at the end of the counter.

"And what secrets do you have?" he asked. This time he couldn't hide the boyish gleam in his eyes.

Though the question shook Jessie to the core, she

quickly recovered, telling herself he wasn't serious. He'd made a joke, and he didn't expect a candid answer.

"There are several secrets." She washed and dried her hands, then leaned against the counter with her hands crossed over her chest. "But a true baker never reveals what makes her special." She quickly corrected her mistake. "Her *bread* special."

Jessie forced a smile and blamed the slip-of-the-tongue on the early hour.

Sliding from the stool, David inched closer. "You will tell me your secrets."

"Or what?" Jessie feigned fright.

"Or I'll tickle you."

Before she could respond, David lunged forward and grabbed her by the waist. Pulling her close, he began to tickle her. Grasping for air between tears and ragged breaths, Jessie begged, "Stop. Stop. I'll tell you anything you want to know."

David kept his hands clasped around her wrists. "Now, that sounds more like it."

Seizing her moment, Jessie easily twisted free. "But it'll cost you."

David shook his head. "I should have known it would."

Pointing a finger at him, Jessie said, "The first rule states you can only share your secrets with someone who works beside you."

"I think you're making this up."

"You're going to learn to bake bread."

David groaned when Jessie grinned. He took a step backward and pointed toward the living room. "I'd better check on Isabel."

Moving quickly, she blocked the doorway. "You're not getting out of here that easily. Besides, it'll be another hour or two before Isabel opens her baby browns."

"You're not going to let me out of this," he said, looking her directly in the eyes.

"Nope." Though she stood her ground, on the inside her heart urged retreat. What had started in fun suddenly made her feel vulnerable.

"You need an apron," she announced, turning her attention from the man to the task.

"I don't think so."

Deciding not to push the apron issue, she set a large and a small glass mixing bowl in front of him. "We'll mix the flour and dry ingredients in the large bowl and the liquids in the smaller. And the yeast—"

"What did you say we're making?" he interrupted.

"Herbed focaccia bread. It's easy enough for a beginner. The cinnamon bread I made is already rising. Though, if you'd like, we could make another batch."

David glanced toward the bread pans and said, "No, the herbed focaccia sounds good."

"I'm surprised you even have bread pans."

"Actually, I use them for meatloaf. Now, if you ever want a mean meatloaf, I'm your man."

Jessie smiled as she measured flour, and David followed her instructions. When it came to the dried herbs, she spooned a specified amount into her bowl and then his.

"I take it this is one of those secrets you're not going to share?"

"Not until you earn my trust."

Standing shoulder to shoulder with her, yet looking straight ahead, David asked, "And how does someone earn your trust?"

The muscles in Jessie's chest tightened and her stomach cramped. She didn't know the answer to his question. She didn't know if she could ever again trust a man with her heart or her dreams.

She tried to swallow, but her throat constricted and she coughed. Even though the question had been asked in jest, her heart felt exposed. Instinctively, invisible walls closed around her. She protected herself in the only way she knew.

She picked up a handful of flour and threw it at David.

With his face and dark red shirt dusted in white, he sputtered, "What's gotten into you?"

Attempting to convey her innocence, she shrugged and stared at him through widened eyes.

"Don't think those pretty green eyes are going to

save you this time,'' he warned. Before she could move, he picked up a handful of flour and tossed it at her face.

She retaliated by dumping a cup of sugar on his head. Before either knew it, a thick haze hung in the kitchen. Their hair and clothes, as well as the countertops and floor, were covered in white.

When the air finally cleared, Jessie and David looked at each other and laughed until they cried, until breathing became labored and they bent over at the waist.

''If I'd known baking was this much fun, I'd have learned how to make bread a long time ago.''

''You don't know the half of what you're missing,'' Jessie quipped.

Their eyes met, and Jessie felt something unexplainable pass between them. In that moment, a fragile thread connected them. She shook her head free of such silly thoughts.

Retreating behind a serious facade, David said, ''I'll help you clean up this mess.''

Ten minutes later, with the help of a handheld vacuum cleaner, a broom and a wet sponge, the kitchen sparkled.

''Now, let's get down to business.''

''You still want to make bread?''

''I'm a man of my word,'' David promised, raising his right hand in Boy Scout fashion.

Maybe David Akers *could* be trusted.

* * *

David sifted flour into a clean bowl, then glanced at the recipe book again before carefully adding sugar, oatmeal, salt and dried milk. Setting the dry ingredients aside, he spooned the yeast into a small bowl, exactly as Jessie had shown him. Letting the tap water run, he tested it with his finger until he felt confident it wasn't too hot or too cold, then he added the water to the yeast and stirred.

Without looking at Jessie, he asked, "How am I doing?"

Dipping her finger into the mixture, she nodded with approval. "So far, so good."

While his hands continued to mix, knead and shape the dough, his mind wandered to more interesting thoughts. Such as how Jessie's hair smelled like jasmine, and the sweetness of her voice as she hummed low and soft while she worked. And how he yearned to wipe the smudge of flour from her forehead and massage her tired shoulders.

And he wondered other things, too—like, why a successful businesswoman seemed so content making bread this early in the morning, why he sometimes caught sadness lurking in her eyes and why Jessie didn't have a half-dozen boyfriends hanging around.

But there was one question he'd quit asking, and that was why she was in his home. Her reasons didn't matter, he told himself. Jessie provided Isabel with the stability, love and nurturing she needed—and that was all that mattered.

Side by side they worked.

She's right, he thought, *I should know how to bake bread.* Though he tried, he couldn't fool himself. His rationale for remaining in the kitchen had nothing to do with good business or improving employee relations—and everything to do with the intriguing woman to his right.

Jessie glanced at him and offered a sly grin. "You're loafing on the job. Pun intended."

"Oh, yeah?" His desire to please her surprised him. Punching the ball of risen dough as he'd just seen her do, he began the second kneading.

When the timer buzzed, David said, "I'll get it."

Pulling on a pair of oven mitts, he opened the oven door and retrieved two loaves of cinnamon bread. "These smell incredible," he said as he placed them on wire racks to cool.

"They came out perfectly," Jessie said, inspecting the golden crust.

David rummaged through a drawer until he located a serrated knife, and then he expertly cut off two steaming slices.

"Butter?" he asked.

"Is there any other way?"

After he smeared a hunk of creamy butter across the bread, he carefully raised it to Jessie's lips. Stepping forward, she took a generous bite. When the melted butter streamed down her chin, he quickly grabbed a paper towel and patted the side of her face.

Jessie licked her lips and pulled away from his touch. "Wow. That's the best bread I've ever eaten."

David took a bite, and while he agreed it tasted delicious, he had to wonder how much his taste buds had been influenced by a certain beautiful woman who ruled his kitchen with her smile.

Looking around at the bread they'd baked, he asked, "What are we going to do with all this?"

Jessie scratched the back of her neck. "We could freeze it."

"But my freezer's already full." David insisted.

"I usually give it to friends and family, but then, I don't usually make this much at one time." Jessie glanced around the kitchen at the loaves of bread.

"We did get a bit carried away."

And though it would probably be a long time, if ever, before he baked another loaf of bread, he hadn't wanted the morning to end. He liked working with Jessie. He enjoyed listening to her chatter about family, church friends and the latest Internet bridal trends.

The realization troubled him. In the past year, he hadn't looked at another woman long enough to have a real conversation. But Jessie was different. She'd made it clear she wasn't looking for a husband, and that had allowed him to relax and let his guard down. In her presence, his heart felt safe.

"If you haven't promised the bread to anyone specific, we can take it over to Hot & Fresh and add it to our daily food bank donation," David suggested.

Jessie's lips parted slightly, and her eyes brightened with admiration. "Hot & Fresh makes a daily donation?"

David nodded. "We donate day-old breads and pastries to several churches and city organizations that serve free meals."

Jessie studied him openly, as if she had free access to his most private thoughts. "By any chance have you ever instructed your bakers to make a little extra bread?"

David poured himself a fresh cup of coffee and sliced another piece of bread. He moved to the breakfast table and signaled for Jessie to join him.

"When it's cold or rainy or a holiday, I send over extra." Revealing his generosity made him uncomfortable. He didn't do it because he needed praise or admiration. He did it because he wanted to feed a hungry person.

"I bet you send over more than a little extra," Jessie pushed.

"Between Isabel and work, I don't have a lot of time for volunteer work. Donating bread isn't much, but it's what I can do."

"You shouldn't apologize. What you do makes a difference. You put food in people's mouths."

David shrugged.

"'Cast your bread upon the waters, for after many days you will find it again,'" she quoted from Ecclesiastes as she tore off a warm chunk of bread and popped it into her mouth.

Cocking his head to one side, David pressed his lips into a straight line. "That scripture never has made sense to me. If I throw bread into the water, I'll get soggy bread. Or the ducks will eat it."

"That's very perceptive." Jessie took another bite of bread. "The point is that what we give comes back to us. You're doing more than just feeding another person. You're telling someone they matter, that they're important, that they make a difference in your life."

"I really hadn't thought of it like that." In fact, until the other night when he'd picked up his Bible and read a few verses, he hadn't given much thought at all to the scriptures. And he wouldn't have that night either except he'd knocked his Bible off the shelf and it had fallen open to Kate's favorite psalm. "You're really making too much out of this."

"I don't think so. You're a good man and a good father. Why are you so shy about letting people see these sides of you?"

David looked away, considering his answer. Daylight illuminated the room, no longer allowing him to hide in the predawn darkness. He glanced at the baby monitor, hoping to hear his daughter's jabbering, but she slept contentedly.

"I like my privacy," he finally admitted.

Jessie hesitated, as if she read *no trespassing* in his eyes, but decided to cross the line anyway. "Who are you hiding from? From yourself? From God?"

"Do you always ask such profound questions before breakfast?"

"You're ignoring me."

He had every intention of walking out of the room, but the sincerity in her eyes stopped him. For reasons he didn't understand, she made him want to confide his fears and hopes.

"Maybe both," he said. "I guess I'm hiding from God."

She nodded thoughtfully, as if she understood the internal turmoil even he couldn't sort out. But it was the empathy in her eyes that compelled him to explain.

"I was raised in a Christian home. I've always believed in God and that He cares about my daily life." He paused as the old pain tugged on his heart.

"But that was before the accident. Before your wife's death." Respect reverberated through Jessie's softly spoken words.

David looked away. Until now, he'd kept this sadness to himself. "Kate's death turned my life upside down and sideways in more ways than I can explain.''

''Not only did you lose your wife, but you lost your trust in God. You no longer knew where or how He fit into your life. Or if He was even still there.'' Jessie took a sip of water, and when he didn't interrupt her, she continued. ''What had once seemed so certain—your purpose and direction in life—was shaken. It became easier to close yourself off from God, your family and friends, rather than risk being hurt again.''

He stared at her with amazement, wondering how she'd been able to sum up so succinctly the many emotions he'd felt but had never been able to verbalize.

Though she was right, he hesitated to confirm her assumptions. ''So you think you've got me all figured out?''

''Sounds like I hit a little too close to home.''

David fought to keep the raging emotions from showing on his face. Suddenly compelled to protect himself, he twisted her observations to suit his needs. ''I don't believe you're talking about me at all. You're talking about yourself.''

Jessie popped another huge piece of bread into her mouth and continued to chew slowly. David raised his eyebrows, proving his willingness to wait on her answer. Taking her time, Jessie followed the last swallow with a sip of coffee.

"What if I *was* talking about myself?" She asked the question as if she were issuing a challenge.

David faltered, uncertain of the best response. If he pursued the subject, he'd be crossing into personal territory. And he didn't think that was wise. The more he learned about Jessie, the more he'd care and the more deeply their lives would become entangled.

Yet, when he looked into her eyes, he wanted to know everything about her. He wanted to know what she thought about raising children and whether she believed there was only one true love for each person in the world. He wanted to know what her hopes and dreams and plans were for the future. He wanted to know if she liked him.

David inhaled deeply, frantically searching his mind for a courteous exit. But before he could say anything, he heard Isabel's sleepy voice over the baby monitor.

"Dada, dada, dada," she called. Her timely cry reminded him that his daughter came first in his life. He didn't have time for romantic notions. He had a child to raise.

"I'd better check on my girl," David said, abruptly ending their conversation.

"As soon as I clean up this mess, I'm leaving for the office," Jessie replied, her eyes heavy with relief.

"I'll see you later."

In the nursery, Isabel's innocent smile cheered his soul. Bending down to pick up her warm, supple body, he hugged her tightly against his chest.

"Daddy loves only you, Isabel. It's just me and you. We were doing just fine before Jessie came along, and I promise we'll do just fine when she leaves."

Chapter Nine

Daddy loves only you, Isabel.

Jessie's body stiffened as she listened to David's voice over the baby monitor as he promised his daughter they would get along fine without her. Gripping the edge of the kitchen countertop, she steadied herself.

Closing her eyes briefly, she tried to imagine her mornings without Isabel's soft cooing or the *swish-swish* of the toddler's legs as she crawled at high speed across the carpeted floors.

But it wasn't just Isabel she'd miss. It was David, too. Or was it the fantasy she'd miss? The ability to wake up each morning and pretend she had a family waiting for her, a family who needed her.

Jessie shook her head. Only yesterday she'd promised her mother she wasn't getting in too deep—and she intended to keep her promise.

After she'd showered and dressed, Jessie slipped out of the house without saying goodbye. As soon as she entered her office, she shoved all thoughts of an energetic toddler into the back corner of her mind and concentrated on business.

Though the hours quickly passed as she worked with her top management team on a new Internet marketing strategy, she had to fight to keep thoughts of Isabel and David at bay. Every time she heard the words *engagement, wedding gift* or *baby shower,* she inwardly cringed. A business that had once anchored her hopes for the future now reminded her of the love missing from her life.

Stop it, she scolded herself, realizing how mired in negative thoughts she'd become. When had she lost all hope? she wondered.

That was an easy question to answer. When the doctor had told her she'd never be able to physically conceive and carry a child, the dream of a family life she'd envisioned had crumbled.

Being sensitive to her disappointment, the doctor had insisted she could always adopt. And she'd believed that was possible...until her fiancé, Garth, had abandoned her shortly after she broke the news to him.

Though he'd made up a flimsy excuse about not being ready to settle down, she knew Garth had left her because she couldn't bear his child. She couldn't blame him, so she didn't fight for their love. Even if she'd convinced him to stay, he would eventually resent her. Children were too important to compromise on. If he couldn't accept her as she was, their relationship would have been doomed from the start.

But if Garth—a God-fearing man who'd said he wanted to spend the rest of his life with her—had deserted her because she was barren, then it could happen again. Any man who married her denied himself of his own flesh and blood.

Jessie clenched her fists, then rose from her chair and stood at the window. Looking out over the James River Expressway, she slowly inhaled and exhaled. Placing both hands over her stomach, she willed herself to calm down and to change the direction of her thoughts.

One thing was certain. Ever since Isabel had stormed into her life, the emptiness in her womb had vanished. Isabel had filled a void in her heart she'd foolishly believed would always exist.

Maybe God had been trying to get her attention. Maybe He'd wanted to show her the futility of her thinking. Was it possible there was a man and a family in her future? Could God have brought Isabel into her life to reawaken the dream?

Hope swelled in her chest, and it frightened her. For so long she'd avoided any romantic involvement with men because she feared being rejected when they discovered the truth. But what if God wanted her to risk her heart again?

She closed her eyes and prayed.

Oh, Lord, I don't know if I dare let myself get close to a man again. I'm too afraid. Will You be there to catch me when I fall? To pick up the pieces if it doesn't work out?

Jessie opened her eyes and watched the late-afternoon traffic stream by. Leaving Isabel in a few weeks would be difficult but not devastating, now that God had restored her hopes.

Jessie worked late into the evening, making up for lost hours. A few minutes after ten o'clock, she packed her briefcase with current files and locked the office door. A growling stomach reminded her she'd been so caught up in work that she hadn't bothered to eat. She considered stopping at a fast-food drive-in, but decided a homemade sandwich and a bowl of vegetable soup sounded better.

Turning into David's driveway, she noticed lights blazing both upstairs and down, and instantly she wondered if something terrible had happened. Isabel's bedtime had long passed, and even David generally turned in early, to be at the deli by 5:00 a.m.

Jessie parked in the garage and quickly entered the house. Throwing her briefcase and blazer on the first chair she passed, she went in search of David and Isabel.

She found them playing in the living room. While Isabel's perky, high-pitched squeals indicated the child had no bedtime thoughts, David's droopy eyes and lips confessed exhaustion.

Though Jessie hadn't made a sound, Isabel looked up as if she'd sensed Jessie's presence. Instantly, the toddler pushed to her feet and with unsteady steps waddled to Jessie. Jessie knelt down and stretched out her arms, as Isabel fell against her chest.

"Do you believe it?" she said. "She walked. She walked to me!"

David's eyes suddenly sparked with newly discovered energy. He wore the proud-papa smile well. Clapping his hands, he gained Isabel's attention. "Come to Daddy."

Isabel hesitated as if she hated to leave the safety of Jessie's arms. Then, reveling in the attention, she slowly walked to her father, teetering from one tiny foot to the other.

David scooped his daughter up in his arms and twirled her around the room. "I was beginning to believe something might be wrong. I've heard more stories of children that walk by nine and ten months than I care to recount."

"You can't second-guess God's timing," Jessie offered, knowing she should listen to her own advice.

"Some things you just can't hurry up. The doctor kept saying that when Isabel wanted something badly enough, she'd walk." Rubbing his daughter's head, David added, "Isn't that right, Pumpkin?"

Isabel clapped her hands as if she knew exactly what she'd just agreed to. Then, eager to practice her new walking skill, she squirmed until David set her down on the floor. Immediately, she headed for Jessie's arms. Though Isabel fell twice, she didn't give up until Jessie held her.

When Isabel wanted something badly enough, she'd walk. David's words rang in Jessie's ears. Isabel had wanted *her.*

Jessie gave Isabel a quick squeeze and then set her down on the floor. Back and forth, the little girl shuffled between her father and Jessie.

With every successful pass, David showered her with kisses and hugs and warm, reassuring words. Raising her head, Jessie met David's gaze. Pure happiness illuminated his dark eyes.

"I'm glad I had someone to share this moment with," he said.

"I wouldn't have missed it for the world."

Touched by his honesty, Jessie swallowed hard. Feeling Isabel tug on her leg, she readily accepted the diversion, picked up the toddler and smothered her neck with kisses.

"What I want to know," she said, interrupting her question with more kisses, which were followed by giggles, "is what you're doing up so late. And don't think that just because you're walking now, you're off the hook."

"She wouldn't go to sleep. I couldn't stand hear-

ing her cry, so I finally gave up and let her play."
He shrugged. "I think she was waiting for you."

Jessie's eyes narrowed with disbelief. "I doubt
that."

David pointed toward his daughter, and when Jessie glanced down at the child in her arms she saw
Isabel's eyes had closed and her breathing had
slowed.

"The excitement of walking wore her out. That's
all," Jessie insisted, though she yearned to believe
otherwise.

"Well, she's asleep now." David's shoulders
hunched with weariness.

"Let me put her to bed," Jessie offered.

"Would you mind? I'll come in to say good-
night."

Jessie carried the sleepy child to the nursery,
where she changed her diaper and exchanged her
sweaty pajamas for a fresh set. After gently laying
her in the crib, she pulled a blanket over Isabel's
chubby body and began to softly hum a lullaby, as
she rubbed her hand over Isabel's head and down
her arm.

Though Isabel quickly drifted off to sleep, Jessie
remained at her side, savoring the precious moment.
When David's footsteps approached, she moved to
make room. They stood next to each other, listening
to Isabel's even breaths as if they were the most
miraculous sound in the world.

Jessie checked the baby monitor, then backed out of the room. David followed.

"I know it's late, but I don't think I can sleep."

"You'll be sorry in the morning," Jessie countered.

"True. Maybe I'll exercise my right as boss and go in a few hours late."

Jessie looked at him skeptically. It would snow in July before David would sleep in on a work morning.

Ignoring her, he added, "I'll bet you didn't take time for dinner."

"How'd you know?"

"I heard your stomach growling earlier."

"I am hungry, but since it's late I'll just grab a light snack. Something quick."

"I've made a pot of decaf. I'll join you."

As soon as she entered the kitchen, Jessie knew exactly what David had been doing while she'd tended to Isabel. It'd been a long time since she'd been pampered, and she could get used to the special treatment.

The table had been set with two place mats, napkins and the everyday china. Three round peach candles burned, filling the room with a sweet aroma. David held her chair out, and Jessie sat down to a turkey sandwich and vegetable soup.

"Did you skip dinner, too?"

"No, but the excitement's made me hungry."

Jessie smiled, replaying Isabel's triumph in her mind. "I had no idea how special a moment like that could be."

"It makes you forget there's anyone else in the world."

"And you're reminded of what's really important—family, friends, faith."

Jessie picked up her spoon, then hesitated. "I'd like to say grace."

David nodded once with approval.

Bowing her head and closing her eyes, she began. "Dear Lord—" her voice faltered slightly as David's hand covered hers "—while we're thankful for this food, we're even more thankful for the joy Isabel brings to our lives. Please, continue to guide her and bless her and protect her as she grows into a woman who hears Your voice. Bless us now as we eat this meal. Amen."

"Amen." David echoed, quickly removing his hand.

Jessie opened her napkin and laid it across her lap. "You really didn't have to go to this trouble."

"It's nothing," he said, making light of the flickering candles and thick sandwiches.

"Maybe so, but it's appreciated."

For a second, they seemed to stumble in silence, and then they both broke in with the same question at the same time. "How was your day?"

"You go first," David insisted.

Jessie quickly recapped a personnel problem and a software glitch, saving the best news for last. "A national women's magazine has requested an interview for a future article."

"That's fantastic," David said. "When will the article run?"

"Not until fall. And I'm not the only one they're interviewing. The article will focus on female entrepreneurs. Sounds impressive, doesn't it?" She dabbed her lips with the napkin, then grinned as if an interview with a national magazine was mundane. But it wasn't. And it wasn't the personal recognition that thrilled her, but the enormous publicity Gifts of Love would receive.

"It is impressive. *You're* impressive."

Jessie smiled, more pleased by the compliment than she liked to admit.

"I know what it takes to make a corporation a success. You've had to put yourself on the line and make sacrifices others wouldn't understand. I admire anyone who's accomplished the things you have."

Jessie's smile stiffened as she sipped the coffee. She'd taken the praise personally. How silly of her. Of course, David would admire *anyone* who'd built a business. He understood and related to the world of management and finance.

"There have been a lot of sacrifices along the way," she admitted. "Do you ever wonder if they're really worth what we gave up?"

David looked away, as if the question were too painful to consider. "We have to believe they are." Then, looking at her, he added, "We don't have a choice. If you live with regrets and what ifs, you'll drive yourself crazy."

"You don't have any regrets?" She found that difficult to believe. She had a zillion regrets. She wished she'd gotten married earlier and had tried to have children before it'd been physically impossible. She wished she hadn't shut God out when she'd needed Him most in her life. She wished...

"Of course I have regrets." For an instant, they flared in his eyes. "But I can't live my life asking *why*. I've got to focus on the future. I have to, for Isabel's sake."

Jessie set down her half-eaten sandwich, selecting her words carefully. "It seems to me that you're not really living your own life. You're living through your daughter."

He jerked back in the chair as if she'd wounded him. Though his face contorted with pain, he maintained his composure. "I think how I choose to live my life—right or wrong—is my own business."

"Of course—" She tried to apologize, but he cut her off before she could finish.

"That little girl asleep in there is the center of my life. She's all I have left from the life I'd always thought I'd have. And I will do everything in my power to make sure she has the happiest and securest life possible. I promised I'd be both mother and father to her, and that I would make up for all that's been stolen from her.''

Jessie allowed David a moment to catch his breath before she responded. "Isabel is a happy, healthy child. It's obvious she feels loved and secure. You've given her more than some children ever have."

David met her gaze, his eyes dark and stern. "But?"

"But, if you continue as you are, you're going to burn out. You have to take care of your needs—"

"Are you telling me I need a woman in my life, that I need to get married in order to be happy?''

Jessie inwardly groaned, praying David didn't think she intended to campaign for the position. "Not at all. Though I expect somewhere down the road you will remarry. You'll want Isabel to have a mother." She sipped the coffee as she redirected her thoughts. "But in the meantime, you have to take care of your heart and soul. You have to find joy and purpose in your life again. In your life here in Springfield. You have to make peace with God. Someday, Isabel's going to grow up and start a life of her own. And then where will you be? Taking care of yourself is a gift you give your daughter.''

David rubbed the back of his neck, pushing his fingers through his short, brown hair. Slowly, a smile came to his face. "I've heard this speech before. Have you been talking to my mother?"

Jessie shook her head, relieved he hadn't been offended by her boldness.

"I'm going to be okay," he promised. "They say time heals all wounds."

"But a push in the right direction never hurts." More than anything, Jessie wished she could help rekindle his joy in life, as well as his faith in God. But then, why did she think she could cure someone else's troubles when she couldn't even fix her own?

David finished his sandwich and shoved the plate to one side. His pursed lips acknowledged the seriousness of his thoughts. "I have to remember that even if Kate had lived, our lives might not have turned out as I believe they would have. I realize I've compared what I have now to an idealized version of what my life once was."

"And that's dangerous," Jessie agreed. Had she done the same thing? Had she created a fantasy of what her life would have been like had she been able to conceive and bear children? Was she constantly comparing what she had to that perfect standard?

David continued. "Kate and I were going to have a house full of children. Well, at least three or four. We were going to take family vacations, and when we grew old we planned to spend the holidays and summers with our grandchildren and great grand-children.''

Desperate to avoid David's gaze, Jessie walked to the other side of the kitchen and poured more coffee into her cup, even though it was still half full. By the way he loved Isabel, she should have known David had wanted lots of children.

"It's a lovely dream," she said, hiding her private distress.

"That's my point. It's a dream. I'll never know if that's the way my life would have turned out." Hope tinged the edges of David's words.

The subtle shift in his voice compelled her to look at him. He sat taller and looked more relaxed. He didn't seem as tired or weary. Could these changes reflect a deeper shift in his heart?

"Why are you looking at me that way?" he asked.

Jessie scratched the side of her head. "If I didn't know better, I'd think..."

"You'd think what?" he prompted.

"I'd think you're starting to like it here in Spring-field."

David rubbed his chin. "I think you're probably right. I just haven't wanted to admit it. It's easier to be angry than to let go of old expectations and dreams.''

Jessie nodded, understanding exactly what he meant.

"So you're not as angry at God?"

David slowly shook his head. "I have you to thank for that."

"Me?" His admission mystified her.

"Yeah, you. You waltzed into our lives with your enthusiasm and joy. You filled this house with your laughter and compassion and generosity. How could Isabel and I not be affected? You've reminded me I have a lot to live for—besides my daughter. Thanks to you, Isabel and I are going to be just fine."

Jessie smiled, truly happy for the heartfelt changes reflected in David's eyes. But while she should have been celebrating with him, she felt suddenly cold and saddened. Witnessing Isabel's eager steps and sharing the late-night dinner—both had lured her into dangerous territory.

This is only temporary, she reminded herself.

Crossing her arms, she shivered.

"Jessie?"

"I'm sorry. What were you saying?"

Instead of answering her question, David fired several of his own. "Where did you go? What did I say to upset you?"

Jessie inhaled deeply but silently. A part of her longed to tell him her thoughts. But another part, a more cautious part of her heart, begged her not to make that mistake.

"You haven't upset me. I'm just tired." She

paused, hoping he'd believe her. "Besides, it's getting late, and you've got an early morning."

"Don't think for a moment you're getting off that easy." David carried his plate and mug to the sink, then leaned against the counter. His mere presence convinced her he wouldn't accept any flimsy excuses in place of the truth.

Jessie grappled with her thoughts. Maybe she could tell David her horrible secret. It would feel so good to share these private emotions with another person. She'd kept them bottled up for too long.

And she felt safe with David, secure he'd understand. After all, he knew what it was like to experience unfair losses. He knew what it was like to question God's ways. But most of all, her life happiness didn't depend on his opinion. He wasn't husband material—at least, not for her. And even if his heart continued to open, he was a long way from letting a woman share his life with Isabel.

As far as she could see, she didn't have anything to lose by confiding. Taking a deep breath, she decided to tell him the truth.

"Three years ago I had an operation..." It had been so long since she'd spoken the words—exposed them to the light of day—that their heaviness twisted her tongue.

When she paused, David didn't try to hurry her. He allowed her time to collect her thoughts and raging emotions.

"Let me back up," she said. "Like you, I'd always pictured my life with a husband and a house full of children. I was even engaged a few years ago."

David reached out to touch her elbow, but before he could offer physical comfort, she pulled back. Not because she didn't appreciate his concern, but because she feared she'd break down before she finished her story. She needed to remain aloof and to tell what had happened as if it'd happened to someone else.

"I'd found the man of my dreams. I believed we'd be together for a lifetime."

Though David furrowed his brow and opened his mouth as if to speak, he didn't interrupt.

"To make a long story short, I became ill, they ran tests and I had an operation."

She stopped again, not sure she could say the words. Because it had been more than just an operation. The physicians had removed much more than a body part. They had excavated the future she'd believed in.

Jessie swallowed and, gathering her courage, looked David directly in the eyes. "I had a hysterectomy."

With his gaze firmly on her, not one muscle in his face twitched. Then he bit down on his bottom lip as if he didn't know how to respond.

But what had she expected him to say? Had she

expected him to take her into his arms, hold her tight and say everything will work out? That we can't always understand God's plans or see the big picture?

She didn't know what she'd expected, but she had counted on more than a blank stare. His silence said what his heart didn't dare reveal. Like her fiancé, he now knew her flaws. She wasn't the complete woman she'd fooled the world into thinking she was.

Jessie raised her chin slightly, desperate to regain her pride. David didn't even love her—and look at the way he'd responded. All her irrational fears came flooding back to her.

Intent on fleeing his penetrating gaze, Jessie took a step back. But just as she turned her back to him, he caught her by the elbow and pulled her close. Now they were face-to-face, and she had no choice but to listen to what he had to say.

"I'm so sorry you had to have a hysterectomy," he finally said.

With David's voice a mere notch above a whisper, she had to lean forward to make certain she'd heard him clearly. Up close, she noticed his dampened eyes. What she saw reflected in his eyes was *her* pain. He felt it, too.

Instantly, she realized she'd misjudged him. She'd unfairly transferred another man's disappointments and doubts to David.

Before she could stop him, his arms reached out and pulled her into an embrace. Safe in his arms, she let fall the tears that she'd held in for so long. In his arms, she no longer felt the need to be brave or to pretend she'd moved past her initial disappointment and disillusionment.

More than ever, she wanted a family.

More than ever, she wanted a man who would love her as she was. A man who wouldn't feel cheated for loving her.

She lost track of time. With her ear pressed against his chest, she found comfort in the steady beat of his heart and the spicy scent of his cologne.

When her tears finally stopped, her vulnerability embarrassed her and she slowly pushed away. Keeping his hands on her shoulders, David didn't let her go far. Tenderly, he ran his hand over her head and down her neck to her shoulder.

"You've lost a lot. Where my loss is obvious, and friends and family have rallied around me with support, you've suffered yours in private."

His sensitivity stunned her.

"But you don't have to go through this alone," he encouraged.

At first she thought he intended to lend his support. Fortunately, before she could say that wouldn't be necessary, she realized he wasn't volunteering for the job.

"My family knows," she explained. "My parents and sisters were with me during the operation."

David regarded her through sage eyes. "But do they realize the wounds have never completely healed? Do they know how much you still hurt?"

She glanced down at the floor on the pretense of evading his question. And she did, for a second or two. Then with deft fingers, he raised her chin and forced her once again to meet his gaze.

"No," she whispered.

"You have to let them in. Don't make the mistakes I made. I tried shutting out my family. But in the end I realized they were the greatest blessing God has ever given me. Let them help you through this."

As she searched his eyes, she knew he had not said all that was in his heart. But his gaze betrayed him by communicating the unspoken: *Let* me *help you through this*.

In an attempt to conceal his true emotions, he rambled on. "Don't push your friends away. And don't push God away. You need Him now more than ever."

Yes, she needed God in a way she'd never needed him before. She was falling for David Akers's smile. And it would take a lot more than prayer to convince her heart to forget him.

Chapter Ten

"Would you pray with me?" Jessie asked. Her voice dropped to a whisper.

She tilted her head down as if she couldn't bear to look him in the eyes, on the chance he'd deny her request.

David hesitated long enough to consider his warring emotions. On one hand, he wanted to pray with her. In fact, he wanted to shout at God to listen to the pleas of this woman's heart. He wanted God to wrap His arms around Jessie and mend her broken dreams. That wasn't too much to ask, was it?

And yet, another part of him didn't want to care about her problems. Jessie wasn't his concern. He wasn't obligated to get involved.

He rubbed his hands together as if the answer to his dilemma might magically appear. When Jessie continued to look down, he thought she patiently awaited his answer. Until he saw her lips move. She'd started to pray without him.

Feeling left behind, David reached out for her hands and drew them into the safety of his grasp. Through her warm touch, he felt both her strength and her weakness.

Joined in silent prayer, the connection between them amazed him. It felt as if an electrical cord stretched between them, and God had flipped the on switch.

"Dear Lord," Jessie prayed. Her voice rang true and sweet, and David wondered if he'd ever heard a sound more tender. "We come to You with troubled hearts. And though we both know we have to let go of our anger and hurt and disillusionment, we don't know how. We've tried it our way, and now we're asking You to lead us through the darkness to Your light."

Determined not to cry in front of Jessie, David fought for composure. The simple, honest prayer came from the heart. She'd said everything he'd tried to express to God but hadn't been able to.

When David opened his eyes and found Jessie staring at him, he realized their friendship had deepened. They could never again claim to be acquaintances passing on a highway. Their lives had become entwined.

"Thank you," he said.

Her glistening eyes probed for an explanation.

David cleared a lump of emotion from his throat. "Thank you for saying the words I've been reluctant to pray."

"I don't deserve your thanks. That prayer was for me."

"Maybe that's why God has brought us together, so we can help each other find our way back to Him."

Jessie nodded, squeezing his hand in affirmation.

David lifted her fingers to his mouth and kissed them, allowing his lips to linger on her smooth skin. When he looked up, his gaze penetrated the protective walls surrounding her heart, and he longed to take her into his arms and kiss her until his lungs begged for air.

Stunned by his desire and eager to escape, David released her hands and backed away. "It's late. We should call it a night."

She nodded and, without another word, left the room without looking back.

In the nanny's bedroom, Jessie fell facedown on the bed and didn't move for a very long time. Resting her forehead on folded arms, she cried. Far removed from the main wing of the house, she didn't worry that David might hear her muffled lament.

It had been a long time since she'd given in to the heartache and had let it flow unrestrained. But now that she'd released the pent-up emotions, she didn't know how to regain control.

After what seemed like a very long time, the tears stopped on their own, and Jessie slid her body off the bed and onto the floor. Kneeling at the side of the bed, she dared to come face-to-face with God and to speak her mind.

"I don't understand the path You've chosen for me. I don't understand why I'll never know the joy of conceiving and bearing a child. I don't know if I will ever feel whole again."

Jessie took a deep breath and, sensing an inner strength she didn't know she possessed, dared to release her grief and anger and look to the future. She'd been so caught up in her disappointment, she hadn't been willing to believe God might have something special planned for the years ahead. Something He'd chosen specifically for her. An extraordinary role only she could fill.

She knew these optimistic thoughts could only have come from God, because her mind was too small, too narrow to believe something so grand.

Locking her fingers together and resting her forearms on the bed, she closed her eyes and began to meditate with an open mind. Slowly, hope mingled with anticipation swelled within her heart. For the first time in too long, she felt the presence of God. He didn't appear with flashing lights or booming thunder. Instead, He came in the quiet peacefulness of a soul still enough to hear His voice and feel His love.

Jessie no longer feared the future. No matter what it held, God would not abandon her. She didn't know where His guidance would take her, but she knew David and Isabel had brought her to this place, and for that, she would always be grateful.

Finally, exhaustion lulled her to a restless sleep.

David stood at the base of the stairs that led to the nanny's quarters and listened to Jessie's sobs. He placed one foot on the bottom step, then halted. Pushing his hands through his hair, he pulled on the dark strands until he could no longer stand the sting.

Swallowing hard, he fought his conscience. Finally, he dropped to the bottom step. He couldn't go to her. It wasn't his place to comfort her. That would only lead her on and make her believe he cared for her in a way he didn't. But he couldn't leave, either. At least, until he knew she was all right. So he sat on the step, prepared to wait for hours until her silence came.

While he waited, he turned his thoughts toward God and prayed. He didn't have much to say, but the sincere words were a start. A series of first steps. Just as Isabel had strung together enough steps tonight to walk across the room with confidence. She'd finally walked because she'd wanted something badly enough. Maybe the same held true for him. He could finally seek God because he was tired of living in exile from the faith he'd once embraced.

Jessie had everything to do with his willingness to reopen communication with God. He admired the way she'd held on to her faith even though she'd questioned God's love. She had come into his life to remind him that as in any relationship, with God there will be times of misunderstanding and turmoil. But this disaccord doesn't mean the relationship ends. Yes, he wanted to be more like Jessie. In the future, he wanted to work through his spiritual crisis instead of turning his back on God when he didn't get his way.

Finally, when Jessie's sobs faded, he returned to the main wing of the house. Pausing at Isabel's doorway, he watched his daughter sleep. How could he have forgotten what a fortunate man he was?

With Isabel still asleep, Jessie prolonged going downstairs. Sequestered in the nanny's bedroom with the baby monitor, she sacrificed her morning coffee to avoid a chance meeting with David in the kitchen. With any luck, he'd be up and out of the house before she descended from the garage quarters.

But Isabel didn't cooperate with Jessie's plans. Awake an hour earlier than normal, Jessie could tell by the toddler's cranky moans that the day was off to a shaky start.

Jessie bounced out of bed and pulled on a pair of blue jeans, then quickly brushed her blond hair and pulled it back into a ponytail. With no time to apply makeup, she didn't even bother looking in the mirror. Besides, she knew what she'd see. Due to lack of sleep, she'd have puffy eyes and dull skin.

Normally, she wouldn't be caught dead in public looking so pale. But this morning she didn't care. It wasn't as if she needed to impress David. In a week or two, she'd be out of here. They might stay in touch as friends, but even that was a long shot. David had made it clear that aside from Isabel and Hot & Fresh, he wasn't willing to make room for anyone else in his life.

Cutting through the garage to the main part of the house, Jessie frowned when she saw David's car still parked in the garage. She crossed her fingers and hoped he was in his bedroom or the kitchen and that she could sneak into Isabel's room and tend to her needs without being noticed.

Jessie quietly eased the nursery door open and, guided by a night-light, stepped into the carpeted room without making a sound. She flipped the light switch, and then jumped when David shouted. Seconds later, Isabel began to cry. David reached down, picked up his freshly diapered daughter and cradled her against his chest.

"Shh. There's nothing to worry about. It's just Jessie—you scared me," David accused.

"I'm sorry," she apologized. "I didn't know you were in here. You're usually at work by this hour."

He shook his head, his irritation showing as darkly as his unshaven beard. Though he didn't speak, his thoughts were clearly written across his tense face: How could Jessie have walked through the garage without seeing his car?

"I decided to go into work late."

That accounted for his disheveled look. If she had to guess, like her, he'd just rolled out of bed. He needed a shower and a cup of extra-strength coffee.

Stepping closer, she rubbed her hand over Isabel's forehead, and the child's tears ceased. When Isabel held out her arms, David relinquished his daughter without hesitation. With Isabel snug against her body, Jessie began to gently bob the child.

"Why don't I fix breakfast while you get ready for work?"

David grunted what Jessie took for a yes.

Though she wasn't hungry, neither was she eager to stand around and chitchat with a grumpy man. For days they'd coexisted comfortably, but last night they'd destroyed their effortless ease. She'd invited David to look too deeply into her heart, and now she regretted sharing her secrets with him. She saw the caution in his eyes, and she felt the awkward tension in the way he avoided bumping into her in the small room as they both tried to leave through the doorway at the same time.

In the kitchen, Jessie secured Isabel in the high chair and then gathered the ingredients to make French toast. But before she could crack the eggs in the mixing bowl, Isabel's pout turned to a scowl and then tears. Unable to bear the little girl's soft cries, Jessie picked her up and rocked her in her arms. As a result, she was forced to abandon plans for a hot meal, so she set cereal boxes and milk on the table. By the time David appeared, the coffee had brewed.

"I intended to make—"

David raised his palms to interrupt her. "It's just as well. I'm not hungry. I'll just grab a cup of coffee and head out."

Seeming anxious, David left the room before realizing he hadn't said goodbye to Isabel. Retracing his steps, he kissed his daughter on the cheek and told her he loved her.

Without looking at Jessie, he called out, "I'll see you later."

"Have a great day."

Jessie listened as the garage door opened and shut, and then she slumped down in a chair. "Well, that went well, didn't it?" she said to Isabel.

In reply, Isabel began to cry, shattering Jessie's hopes that the day would get better.

Three hours later, with Isabel still fussy, Jessie reached the end of her rope. She'd tried everything she knew to comfort, amuse and distract the toddler. But nothing had worked. Isabel wasn't interested in her favorite toys. She asked for juice, then threw the bottle on the floor. She didn't want to be held, but neither did she want to play on the floor or in her crib.

When Jessie had exhausted her own knowledge and common sense, she flipped through a half-dozen child-rearing books. But they hadn't supplied any magical answers. Finally, in desperation she called her sister Maria.

Before she could even enquire about Maria's health, her sister asked, "What's wrong?"

"I sound that bad?"

"Afraid so."

"I look worse."

When Maria laughed, Jessie joined her. By poking fun at herself, she released some of the tension.

"I'm sorry I haven't stopped by or called lately. Mom said you've been doing fine."

"Don't worry, sis. Between Mom and my mother-in-law, I've got more help than I can stand."

They laughed again, not because it was funny but just because they knew each other so well that they often communicated more by not saying anything.

"I hear you have your hands full," Maria said.

"Little Isabel is more than I can handle today." Jessie looked down on the sweet face, wondering how those tender brown eyes could produce so many tears, and then filled Maria in on Isabel's behavior.

"My guess is that she's just having a cranky day," Maria said. "Welcome to motherhood."

"So, I shouldn't call the doctor?" Jessie had been ready to rush to the emergency room.

"I'd keep a close watch on her for the rest of the day, but I don't think there's anything wrong with her."

"So what do you do with my sweet nephew when this happens?"

"First, I forget about getting anything done for the rest of the day. Then I bundle Kraig up and take him for a car ride. And if I'm really, really lucky, riding in the car lulls him to sleep—and when he wakes up with a smile on his face it's a whole new world."

"Thanks, Maria. You've saved my day." With her hope renewed, Jessie hung up the telephone.

Jessie changed Isabel's diaper and clothes, then fastened her into the car seat. But after a half-hour of driving the back roads south of Springfield, pointing out all the pretty spring flowers, puppy dogs and school buses they passed, Isabel had yet to crack a smile.

Frazzled, Jessie decided to go home. Then, at the last minute, she pulled onto the expressway and drove straight to the Hot & Fresh corporate office.

The one-story redbrick building occupied a large grassy lot on a busy street. Pin oak trees and box-wood shrubs lined the front sidewalk, creating a cool, shady entrance. The beginnings of a smile perched on Isabel's lips as they passed through the familiar front door. Jessie's instincts were right on target. Finally.

The comfortable elegance of the reception area impressed Jessie. Green marble floors, oil landscapes and deep tan leather sofas exuded success. Walking over to a tall crystal vase of fresh-cut flowers, Jessie and Isabel inhaled the sweet fragrance of stargazer lilies and roses. In the distance, the chatter of employees created an energetic buzz. Everywhere she glanced, she saw David's heart and soul.

Before she could ask the receptionist to see David, the grandmotherly woman ran around her desk to greet Isabel. Within seconds, several employees surrounded Jessie. They were as happy to see Isabel as the toddler was to see them. But it wasn't until David appeared from down the hallway that Isabel squealed with glee and waved her tiny fists through the air.

When David took his daughter, Jessie felt a huge wave of relief. Tilting his head quickly to one side, David indicated for Jessie to follow him. As she matched his steps, she felt the gazes of curious people on her back.

As she'd expected, David's office decor mirrored the reception area. With one exception. A playpen and toy box occupied the far corner of the spacious room. And as happy as Isabel had been to see her father, she quickly eased from his grasp and toddled over to her toys. She plopped herself down and, with a crazy grin on her face, rediscovered dolls and balls and books she'd forgotten she had.

Staring at Isabel, Jessie pressed her fists against her waist and said, "Well, I'll be. I wish I'd figured out what she wanted three hours ago."

David covered his mouth in an attempt to stifle a chuckle, but failed. Jessie playfully punched him in the arm. "You think this is funny?"

And even though she thought it was, too, she had to fight back tears. She wasn't about to let David see how stressed she'd become.

"Running a corporation is a lot easier that raising a toddler."

"Isn't that the truth." When she met David's steady eyes she felt as if they'd created a memory that would never be forgotten. One of those moments stored forever in the life albums of the mind. With every day that passed, they created a new page of history. With every day that passed, they became a little closer.

Turning serious, David said, "Listen, I know you said you wanted to watch Isabel until Elaine returned, but if you've changed your mind, I can find—"

Jessie stubbornly shook her head. "I keep my promises. Today was just a temporary setback. I'm a little slow with the toddler lingo. But I'm learning."

As if they were more than friends, David placed his arm around Jessie's shoulder and squeezed her tightly. Oblivious to the way their bodies fit so closely together, they watched Isabel play, enjoying the companionship.

However, it didn't take long for the warnings to creep into Jessie's mind. David's arm suddenly became very heavy, and Jessie slipped from his side. "We shouldn't interrupt your day any further. I'm sure you have a lot of work to do."

She knew *she* did. The plan to care for Isabel and manage Gifts Of Love, hadn't gone as well as she'd hoped. She wasn't superwoman.

"My day's not too busy," he continued. "I just had an appointment cancel." David walked over to his desk and opened a day organizer. With his lips pressed together in concentration, he confidently ran his finger down a long list. Then he picked up the telephone and buzzed his assistant. "I'm clearing my schedule for the next couple of hours.... Oh, I'd forgotten about that. Abram can handle that....yes, reschedule Fulcrum for later in the week."

Suddenly Jessie didn't feel so bad for putting off work at Gifts of Love. She'd bet David had plenty to do. But he, too, found a certain toddler irresistible at times. And if David wanted to spend the afternoon with his daughter, that would free her up to spend the afternoon at her office.

Scooping Isabel up in his arms and tickling her, he said, "What would you girls think about a picnic?"

The invitation surprised her. Especially in light of the awkwardness earlier in the morning. But how could she say no?

Against her better judgment, Jessie accepted. "I think it's a fabulous idea. I couldn't think of a nicer way to spend the day than with my two favorite people."

The words popped out before she could edit them. And when David seemed not to notice, she chose to act as if she hadn't revealed the intimate secret. Instead, she focused on Isabel. Reaching out, she tickled Isabel until the little girl giggled uncontrollably. But when she sneaked a glance at David's deep eyes, she knew her innocent remark still resonated in his heart.

Chapter Eleven

David shook the quilt in the air and let it settle—accidentally on purpose—over Isabel's head.

While Isabel batted the underside of the hand-stitched quilt, David called out, "Where's Isabel hiding?"

When he peaked under the family heirloom, he said, "There she is." Innocent laughter rewarded his efforts.

Still holding the picnic basket ten minutes later, Jessie said, "I hate to stop all the peek-a-boo fun, but I'm hungry."

"What do you think, Pumpkin? Is it time to eat?" David asked his daughter.

Both he and Jessie interpreted Isabel's energetic string of syllables as a "yes."

Together, David and Jessie spread out a variety

of Hot & Fresh sandwiches, fruit salad and pastries. While David poured two iced mocha lattes into plastic cups, Jessie fed Isabel.

"Mmm," Jessie said as she spooned the last bite of applesauce into Isabel's open mouth. "Mmm, mmm, good."

"It's amazing how quickly a toddler can ruin a perfectly good vocabulary." David leaned back on one arm, his long legs stretched out in front of him. He chose a thick corned beef sandwich on wheat and took a generous bite.

"Not to mention what it does to your wardrobe. I immediately went from power suits, hose and heels to jeans, T-shirts and sneakers."

Jessie smiled as she put Isabel on a blanket to drink her bottle. Sitting in the park on a warm, sunny spring day was exactly what she'd needed to soothe her harried nerves.

As she sipped the icy latte, she struggled to find the right words. Setting her turkey sandwich aside and hugging her knees to her chest, she said, "I want to apologize for this morning."

Without hesitation, David shook his head. "No, I should be the one to apologize."

Silence filled the distance between them. Jessie glanced at David and immediately sensed that his thoughts echoed hers. He, too, wondered if it would be wise to delve into the matter any further. Some things were better left unsaid.

But Jessie needed to explain. "I said things to you last night that I didn't expect to confide, and it's left me feeling a little vulnerable."

"If you're worried I'm going to tell anyone—"

"No, it isn't that," she said, finding it easier to focus on the latte than on David. "I'm just not used to spilling my guts to someone I barely know."

"Well, I wouldn't say we barely know each other. You can't live under the same roof with someone and not get to know them quickly."

Jessie found the justification plausible. "I guess you're right."

Sitting up, his legs crossed at his ankles, David studied Jessie for a moment, forcing her to meet his gaze. "What's really troubling you?"

She couldn't believe he could be so dense. Did she have to be blunt? "I'm afraid I might have given you the wrong idea."

"The wrong idea?"

"Yeah." Jessie sat back on her heels. She regretted pushing the conversation in this direction. They obviously weren't on the same wavelength anymore. Thank goodness. "It was nothing," she said, hoping he'd let it drop.

"Please, I'd like to know what you were thinking." Sincerity darkened his brown eyes.

Jessie cleared her throat and took a deep breath. "By confiding in you, I thought you might think I was trying to get closer to you."

"Oh," David said.

Though he sounded surprised, she had a funny feeling the idea wasn't new to him. "I want you to know, I'm not interested in you." She stumbled over the words. "I like being your friend, and I wouldn't want you to think I had any hidden intentions."

David glanced at his daughter, whose eyes fluttered with sleep. "'Hidden intentions.' Like making a temporary situation permanent?"

"Exactly," Jessie said. Humiliation stroked her cheeks and made her want to crawl under the patchwork quilt and hide. Why couldn't she have let the subject drop when David gave her the opportunity?

"There's no need to explain. You know I'm not in the market for romance or a wife—though for Isabel's sake..."

Was he saying he would marry someone he didn't love, to give Isabel a mother? Before she could form a question, he continued.

"I understand why you're here, Jessie."

The tender way he spoke her name compelled her to look at him. "You do?"

"I figured that out last night."

She waited for him to continue, curious to hear the conclusions he'd drawn.

"That night at the hospital, when you offered to stay with Isabel, I thought you were just being nice. But when you insisted on watching her until Elaine returned, I knew something else motivated you."

"You didn't buy my Good Samaritan act?" The pitch of Jessie's voice climbed a notch as she clung to the tiniest hope he might still be persuaded to think she'd acted out of pure generosity.

"No, I didn't. However, that's not to say I don't think what you've done is extremely kind. Not to mention, you saved the day, so to speak. But you haven't been burning the candle at both ends, juggling Isabel and your business all to help me out. You're also doing this for yourself."

Jessie looked down at the bright-colored patches of fabric, and traced the random seams with her fingertip. Her life resembled this quilt, she thought. Unlikely pieces stitched together in a crazy, unpredictable pattern.

When David cleared his throat, Jessie looked up. "That makes me sound selfish," she said, uncomfortable with his observation.

"I suppose," David agreed. "But *selfish* is not a word I'd use to describe you."

More than anything, Jessie wanted to ask him what words he would use to describe her. Would he say she was *beautiful? Energetic? Intelligent? Compassionate? Funny? A woman of faith?* Knowing she cared what he thought disturbed her more than she wanted to admit.

Resting his hand briefly on her wrist, he said, "I'm just thankful you've been here for me and Isabel. We haven't had an easy time lately. Well...and the way she's taken to you has made me open my eyes."

This time David turned away. Jessie burned with curiosity, wondering what her presence could have forced him to admit.

"How?" she asked.

"For so long I've been trying to be both mother and father to her. I thought I was doing a pretty fair job, until you came along and I began to see how much Isabel is truly missing."

Surprised by the admission, Jessie narrowed her eyes. "But you've got Elaine, and from what I hear she's wonderful with Isabel."

"Elaine is wonderful." David twisted a sandwich wrapper between his fingers as he spoke. Looking deep into Jessie's eyes, he said, "I don't know how to explain the difference. While Elaine loves Isabel, she's never been more than a nanny. But you..."

When Jessie saw the pain in his eyes, she wondered if he'd continue.

"...you've been the mother I always believed Kate would have been. I'm not saying you're like Kate," he quickly added.

"I think I understand."

"When I see you with Isabel, I see a mother holding a daughter. It's the way you talk to her, the way you anticipate her moves, the way you rock her to sleep."

Jessie closed her eyes. *Isabel's mother.* How she

wished that were true. But it wasn't. And she didn't know if she would ever be any child's mother.

"Taking care of Isabel isn't a game for me." She wanted to be clear on that issue. "I'm not some crazy woman who's come into your house. Someone who doesn't know fact from reality." Jessie felt her blood pressure rise with each word. He had to understand.

"Shh," David said. "I don't think you're crazy."

Jessie looked down at the bright quilt, then over at Isabel. David leaned closer, gently tugging her hands into his grasp. She fought the urge to look at him, not willing to take the chance that she'd see pity in his brown eyes. She wouldn't be able to stand that.

"You've been hurt. Deeply. That I understand. And if Isabel helps ease or heal your pain, I think that's wonderful. I think we all win."

Still holding his hand, Jessie dared to gaze into his eyes. Relief flooded her heart as she beheld respect and empathy.

"What do you get out of all this?"

Did he secure more from their temporary arrangement than the knowledge that his daughter was well cared for? Was it possible their friendship had changed his heart in some way?

These were dangerous thoughts. And even more dangerous was the prospect that he considered making a permanent place in his life for her. Would he ask her to marry him, for his daughter's sake?

Jessie couldn't stop herself from exploring the possibilities. From the beginning, she'd believed God had brought her and Isabel together for a purpose. She hadn't allowed herself to wonder what David might gain from their meeting.

Fortunately, David ended her speculation before it could get out of hand. "You've shown me what I've been too stubborn to accept. My daughter needs more than a nanny. She needs a mother."

"Given time, you'll fall in love."

Dropping her hands, David shook his head and looked away. "No. I'll never allow that to happen."

"But..." Jessie let the objection fade to silence. She understood clearly what he'd said. He would marry for Isabel, but not for love.

A few seconds passed before David turned around, and when he did, the forced optimism in his expression didn't fool Jessie. She prayed for words that would ease his mind. But before she could pull her thoughts together, a cold determination frosted his eyes, and she realized the subject was no longer open for discussion. Admitting the truth was not the same thing as acting upon it.

In an attempt to get the conversation back on track, she swallowed nervously and said, "I'm glad you really understand why I wanted to be with Isabel. I don't have anyone I can talk to about this.

My closest friends all have children. Though they sympathize, they can't really know how I feel.''

"What about your family? You said you told them and that your parents and sisters had been at the hospital with you when you had surgery."

Though it was painful to talk, Jessie continued. She needed to vent her frustrations and heartache. Holding it in only intensified her sorrow and pain, causing it to fester and grow.

''They've been wonderful. But—'' Jessie exhaled loudly ''—but I don't feel like I can truly let them see what's in my heart.''

"Because of your sister's pregnancy?"

Jessie nodded her head, thankful for his sensitivity. "I wouldn't want to chance putting a damper on my sister's joy. And if she knew the pain I sometimes feel when I hold my nephew or when she puts my hand on her stomach so I can feel the unborn child kick, it would break my sister's heart. I don't want her to worry about me. I want to celebrate with her and enjoy each day as we await the birth. And I am happy for her. I hope she has a half-dozen children. A dozen children!"

David smiled. Releasing one hand, he reached up and caressed the side of her face. "You're an amazing woman, Jessie Claybrook. I've never met anyone like you."

The affection in his voice compelled her to meet his gaze again. What she saw both elated and confused her. Could he be starting to think of her as more than just a friend?

No, she couldn't believe that. And his next comment clarified her doubts.

"A wonderful woman like you deserves to be married. Someday, you and your husband will adopt a house full of children. There are abandoned children out there who would blossom with your care and love."

Jessie released his hand and scooted to the edge of the blanket. She should have been relieved he didn't think of her in a romantic light. But she wasn't. She was strangely disappointed.

While she appreciated his compliment, she still found herself comparing David to her former fiancé. Automatically, she pictured Garth's face and heard his final rejection. *A man wants to have his own children,* he'd admitted in a heated argument. While there were plenty of men who would be willing to adopt, she always seemed to fall in love with men who couldn't see past her inadequacy. And whether or not David ever fell in love with her, he'd never offered a hint as to whether he'd be willing to love an adopted child.

"Oh, Jessie," David said, seeming to suddenly realize the troubling impact of his words.

Not trusting herself to speak, she shook her head and raised her hands to indicate she was okay, that he needn't worry about her.

David pushed his fingers through his hair and grunted. ''I meant it as a compliment. I'm sorry I've upset you. Give me a minute to get my foot out of my mouth, and then I'll try to explain what I really meant to say.''

Jessie offered a slight smile, and David slumped with relief.

As he gathered his thoughts, reality blanketed Jessie as surely as if someone had thrown the family quilt over her head. She couldn't deny the truth any longer. The lines between reality and fantasy were so blurred she'd lost her bearings. Though she kept telling herself she could walk away from Isabel and David in a few weeks and be thankful for the time she'd spent with them, leaving Isabel would break her heart.

She couldn't love Isabel more if she'd given birth to her. And David, well, she really didn't know what she felt for him. Could she be falling in love with him? No, she didn't think so. But she hated to think she cared for him simply because he was Isabel's father.

Whatever the case, Jessie had to take a long, honest look at her situation. She wasn't Isabel's mother. David wasn't in the market for a wife. In a few weeks, she'd walk out of their lives.

Oh, Lord, she silently prayed, *please help me find the strength to let go.*

But pride prevented her from admitting all this to

David. Instead, she tried to gloss over her true feelings. "When I meet the right man, we'll get married and adopt."

If only she could believe it would be that simple.

But as she waited for David's explanation as to what he'd meant earlier, it occurred to her that when she did fall in love, she wanted a man like David. A man who loved his family above all else. A man who was as prosperous in his relationships as he was in his career. If she was lucky, she just might fall in love with a man like David.

"Trust me, they'll be lining up for you." David leaned back, widening the growing distance between them.

"Yeah, right." Jessie laughed.

When David didn't laugh and his countenance turned serious, she bit down on her lip and waited for him to speak.

"Did you ever consider that the problem is in you, not in the person you love?"

She glared at him, wondering how she could have misjudged him. He obviously didn't understand her feelings at all. "Of course the problem is with me. I'm the one who can't have a child. I'm the one who isn't whole."

David stared at her, unwilling to compromise his position. "That's exactly what I'm saying. You're the one who thinks you're not whole. You're the one who sees yourself as inadequate."

"Oh," Jessie said, letting the deep meaning of his words sink in.

Inching closer, David continued. "When I look at you, I see a beautiful woman of faith. A woman with a heart full of love. A woman with confidence and purpose in life."

Jessie tried to think of something to say, but the words stuck to the roof of her mouth.

"What do you see when you look in the mirror? Do you see what I see, Jessie? Or do you see a woman with a missing piece?"

Unable to shake the image he'd painted, Jessie looked down at the quilt. Somehow its many pieces fit together in a perfect yet crazy pattern. Maybe instead of seeing herself as damaged, as a woman without a womb, she needed to see that her pieces just fit together in a different way. There was nothing wrong with the quilt of her life. God had just selected a unique pattern for her.

"I want to see what you see," she finally said.

"That's a start. You've had some bad experiences in the past. You can't judge all men by your former fiancé. I know, without a doubt, that you're going to meet a man who will fall in love with you, and when that happens adoption won't be an issue. He'll want to adopt children with you. Lots of children."

Jessie started to relax a little. "You guarantee that?"

"You bet," David said.

"You ever think about being a coach?"

David just laughed.

"I'm serious. You're great with pep talks."

"This is more than a pep talk. I mean what I say."

"Because you have to believe it, too?" Jessie asked, with a flash of insight.

David raised his brows as if he didn't have a clue what she meant.

"In a way, we're in the same boat. The woman you fall in love with is going to have to love Isabel as if she were her own. She's going to have to want to adopt your daughter. You're a package deal."

Too late, Jessie realized the fallacy of her theory. When David married it wouldn't be for love.

Rushing on, in an attempt to avoid further embarrassment, she added, "It's easier to imagine things working out for someone else than for yourself."

"That's the truth." David glanced at his daughter when he heard her stir.

Isabel stretched her pliant arms over her head and opened her sleepy eyes. Rolling over, she crawled into Jessie's lap.

Jessie, wishing for something that would never be hers, kissed the child's forehead.

David wasn't surprised, but he was relieved when Jessie called that evening to say she'd be working late and not to expect her until after dinner.

He fed Isabel, put her to bed and welcomed the solitude.

Reclining in his favorite chair, he began a mystery novel he'd been looking forward to reading. But after rereading the opening pages several times, he set the book aside. Then he switched on the TV. When that didn't satisfy him, he tried listening to his favorite CDs. In a distant part of the house, a clock chimed, reminding him of the late hour. Still, he didn't go to bed. Even though he felt tired, he was too restless to sleep.

Too many thoughts swirled in his mind.

Too many thoughts of Jessie.

He should never have allowed her to come into his home. It had been a mistake. He could see that clearly now. Little by little, she'd invaded his and Isabel's lives, and everywhere he looked he saw her fingerprints.

Why he hadn't noticed them before, he wasn't sure. Maybe he hadn't wanted to notice. Her personal touch was undeniable.

Her fiery fragrance lingered in the air long after she'd left the room. Begonias and impatiens she'd planted bloomed in the front flower beds. She'd reorganized the kitchen cupboards and pantry, making more efficient use of the space. Throughout the house, pictures and accessories had been rearranged, and a few items he'd never seen before—baskets with silk flowers, embroidered sofa pillows, and an arrangement of gilt-framed Monet prints—had suddenly appeared on walls and tables. A photograph she'd taken of Isabel had been framed and added to the mantel collection. Candles and fresh floral bouquets added warmth and color to the house.

In a few weeks, Jessie had transformed his house into a cozy home. Where he'd once just looked forward to seeing his daughter's smile after work, he now looked forward to spending time here. She'd created a nest, a secure place for him to begin and end each day.

And there had been other unexpected benefits. The more he settled in at home, the more he felt centered in his heart and the more interested he became in the world around him. For the many months since his wife's death, he'd been stuck in a depressive haze, letting life swirl around him. Then Jessie had come along and had reached out a hand and said, *Come back to your family and friends.*

She'd planted a seed of hope in his heart that had taken root and made him feel alive again. Each day, this new joy and peace crowded out a little more of the anger and bitterness he harbored toward God. He still didn't understand why he'd had to lose so much, but he was beginning to see that if he didn't give his heart back to God he might lose even more.

Isabel deserved a father who could teach her how to make peace with God.

And Isabel deserved a mother. But he wasn't willing to take that step yet. He'd barely survived the loss of his wife. Though for Isabel's sake he wouldn't put marriage off forever, he couldn't put himself or his daughter in that position so soon. Their hearts were still too vulnerable.

For a little while longer, he'd have to be enough for Isabel.

Oh, Lord, he prayed, *don't let my daughter suffer for my inadequacies. I know she needs a mother, and for that reason I'm thankful You've sent Jessie into our lives for this short time. But now it's time for her to go back to her life.*

When he opened his eyes, he knew what he needed to do.

He needed to keep his distance from Jessie. The romantic signals he sensed from her weren't real. Being under one roof for so long had created a false sense of nesting. He told himself that once Jessie moved home, everything would change between them. They'd both get caught up in their everyday lives, days would fly by, and he wouldn't even think of her.

Feeling sleepy, he considered going to bed. Instead, he turned on the stereo and mindlessly listened to CD after CD. He dozed in the chair, waiting for Jessie to come home. Not because he missed her company, he told himself, but because he wanted to make sure she arrived safely.

The sound of the garage door awakened him. As he suspected, Jessie went directly to the nursery to check on Isabel. Intending to say a quick good-night before he shuffled off to bed, he sought her out.

When he reached the doorway of Isabel's room and saw Jessie's silhouette in the dim shaft of light, he sucked in his breath. As beautiful and ethereal as an angel, her love for Isabel overwhelmed him. Seeming to sense his presence, she turned and looked at him. Even in the pale light, her eyes glowed with affection. She smiled, and without hesitation he ignored his recent resolve and moved toward her.

Standing behind her, he softly placed his hands on her shoulders and joined Jessie as she recited a prayer he remembered from childhood.

"Now I lay you down to sleep. I pray the Lord your soul to keep. If you should die before you wake, I pray the Lord your soul to take."

After they prayed, Jessie leaned forward to tuck the blanket around Isabel's precious body. Then she kissed the toddler on the forehead and lovingly smoothed her fingers across the top of the child's head and down the side of her cheek.

When Jessie straightened, David's hands slipped down her arms. Inching closer, he pressed his chest against her shoulders and, clasping his hands on the crib railing, tightened his embrace. The moment felt so natural. He longed for the sweet comfort Jessie's company offered. He'd been on his own so long, he didn't realize how wondrous it would be to share his daughter's special moments.

Aware of a slight shift in Jessie's body, David anticipated the turn of her head. When she looked up at him and blessed him with a smile, he swallowed hard. Though he knew he should back away gracefully, his feet remained firmly planted on the floor. Ignoring all caution, he pressed his lips lightly against Jessie's. When she clutched him tightly, he deepened the kiss. She made him feel as if he were climbing the highest mountaintop. She made him feel as if he could fly. She made him feel lucky to be alive.

When he paused for air, he looked into her eyes, and he saw the confusion, as well as the questions he couldn't answer. How could he be so careless? How could he lead her on?

Taking her by the hands, he slowly pulled her into the hallway. There in the light, reality struck him.

"I'm sorry," he mumbled. "That should never have happened. We were both exhausted."

Jessie nodded once, very slowly. Then she turned and walked away, her carriage stiff but proud.

He considered going after her, but decided that would only complicate matters. For if she looked too closely into his eyes, she'd know he had lied.

He wasn't sorry.

He wasn't sorry one bit.

He had wanted to hold Jessie. He still longed to hold her. And what disturbed him the most was that he hadn't thought of his late wife once while Jessie had been in his arms. He hadn't been looking for a replacement or someone to be Isabel's mother.

He'd been looking for Jessie.

Chapter Twelve

When Jessie woke the next morning, she still felt the heat from David's hands on her skin and the warmth of his breath on the base of her neck. Sleep had neither dulled nor muted the vivid memory. His apology echoed in her mind.

Only when she recalled the regret in his eyes did the intense emotions flee.

She was sorry, too. Sorry she'd have to face him. Sorry she'd have to find a way to convince him she'd simply been swept away on a foolish whim.

But here in the solitude of first light, she somehow found the courage to speak the truth to God. She could have eased out of David's embrace. But no, she'd stepped into the fantasy. For a moment, she'd lived a role that wasn't hers.

And being a wife and mother felt every bit as incredible as she'd always dreamed it would feel.

With her hands clasped and her eyes closed, Jessie continued to pray. *I know this isn't my home, Lord. That Isabel isn't my daughter and David isn't my husband. Forgive me for taking what wasn't mine. Help me to set aside my own desires and to fulfill Your purpose while I'm here.*

Jessie softly said, "Amen," then opened her eyes. Still on her knees, she continued to reflect on the previous evening. There'd been remorse in David's eyes—a sense he'd started something he couldn't finish. But there'd been something else. In the dim light, she hadn't trusted her senses. Was it possible he hadn't kissed her out of mere curiosity or momentary desire? Was it possible he felt drawn to her? Maybe even was falling in love with her?

Firmly, Jessie nipped the ridiculous thoughts. From the beginning, David had made it clear he had no plans to fall in love. His daughter—not his heart—was his sole priority. When he married it wouldn't be for love, and she would never settle for less than love.

Jessie crossed her hands over her chest and wondered how she'd managed to get so involved with David's life. She certainly hadn't been thinking with the brain God had gifted her with. From now on, she would focus on Isabel. God had chosen her to care for the little girl, and she wasn't going to let Him down.

At the office, Jessie planned to work late. Or at

least until after David retired for the night and
there'd be no chance of bumping into him in the
house. But early in the evening, she realized she'd
left a file on her makeshift desk—David's dining
room table—and she couldn't proceed without it.

Still clinging to the hope David had already fed
Isabel and put her down to sleep, she entered the
house intent on grabbing a quick snack and then
diving into work.

But luck wasn't on her side.

She walked in as David lifted Isabel into her high
chair and secured the safety belt. Immediately, the
toddler blinded her with a hundred-watt smile, and
Jessie's resolve to make a quick exit was dashed.

"Have you eaten yet?"

Tension lurked behind David's polite offer. Obviously, he was willing to act as if last night's kiss
had never happened. And if he could put the kiss
behind him, then she could, too.

Concerning dinner, she considered telling a white
lie. But if she said she'd eaten, then she'd have to
forgo the snack, and before she could commit one
way or the other her stomach growled.

As she shrugged, she said, "I am hungry. I lost
track of time at the office."

"There's plenty to eat," he said without looking
at her, setting his plate of grilled chicken, wild rice
and steamed broccoli at her place. Without a word,
he returned to the kitchen for a second plate. Fol-

lowing a few steps behind him, Jessie entered and filled two glasses with water, and at the last minute added a slice of lemon to each.

The expansive kitchen suddenly seemed too small, too cozy, as each time she turned around she bumped into David.

"Sorry," she said, moving out of his way, as he reached for a loaf of bread and sliced off generous pieces.

Jessie grabbed the butter from the refrigerator, praying they'd find a way to thaw the awkwardness between them over dinner.

But her prayers went unanswered. When they weren't talking baby talk to Isabel, they sat in silence. What could she say to him? Anything except the weather seemed too personal. And how many different ways could she praise the grilled chicken?

Believing she'd choke on the next bite if something didn't change, she nearly jumped with joy when the doorbell rang. Before David could push his chair back, Jessie rushed past him.

She peeked through the frosted glass panel before unlocking the dead bolt. Pressing her hand over her heart, she thanked God for sending help. Never had she been so glad to see her sister Maria.

"Come in," she said, hugging Maria.

"I should have called first," Maria apologized. "But I had to run an errand out this way, and so when I detoured through the neighborhood and saw the lights still on, I decided to stop.''

''Nonsense,'' David said as he welcomed her into the house. ''As long as Jessie's here, you're always welcome to drop by.''

But I won't be here much longer, Jessie thought.

''Oh, you're eating.'' Maria stopped abruptly.

''We're just about through. Why don't you join us for a cup of hot tea and dessert?'' Jessie quickly offered, anxious for her sister to stay.

''Well.'' Maria hesitated, rubbing the small of her back with her knuckles. ''It does sound like an offer that's too good to be true.''

''You look like a woman in need of a little pampering.'' David took her arm and nudged her forward. Pulling out a chair, he helped her deposit her very pregnant body squarely onto the seat. Then he disappeared into the kitchen.

''You're sure I'm not interrupting anything?''

Jessie answered for both her and David. ''Not a thing.''

''Just a quiet family dinner,'' he said, reappearing in the doorway with a steaming cup of tea. ''It's chamomile. It'll soothe your soul. Or at least that's what Kate always claimed.'' The last few words were spoken so softly that Jessie knew Maria didn't hear them. But she understood his message. No one would ever replace his wife.

''And if you'll excuse me,'' David quickly added,

"I'm going to put this little one to bed, and let you girls talk."

David lifted Isabel out of the high chair, and with his daughter securely in his arms he paused briefly in front of Jessie, allowing her to kiss Isabel good-night.

"She's darling." Then with a gleam in her eyes, Maria said, "And I bet she's a handful."

"She sure is." Love and longing merged in Jessie's tone. "But you didn't come here to talk about Isabel, did you. There's something on your mind."

When Maria sighed, her entire body expanded. "You always could see through me."

"It works both ways."

"For the record, I do have a legitimate reason for stopping by. Mom and Dad are hosting a family baby shower for me and John. It's kind of impromptu. It was Dad's idea."

"And a good excuse for Mom and Dad to have a party."

"Exactly. Anyway, it's going to be at the lake house next Sunday."

"Great. I'll be there."

But the way her sister's lips parted signaled there was more to the invitation.

"Mom and Dad want to make sure David and Isabel are invited. They also expect us all to attend church as a family."

"O-oh." Jessie stretched the word with dismay.

"I'll ask David. I hope you won't take this personally, but I don't think he'll want to come."

"Be sure and invite him, because I'd count on a follow-up invitation from Mom."

Jessie rolled her eyes. "What's the deal? Doesn't this family trust me to issue an invitation?"

Maria looked directly at Jessie and said, "Come on, sis. You've practically moved in with David. We've hardly seen or talked to you since the tornado. Of course, we're all a little curious."

Jessie pushed her shoulders back, astonished by the implication. "For your information, there's nothing inappropriate going on here. The nanny's apartment is at the far end of the house. And as for not talking to you, I am sorry for that. I've just been so busy. Between work and Isabel…I had no idea what I was getting into when I offered to watch her. I thought it'd be a cinch to juggle a toddler and a business."

"Whoa." Maria waved her hands to signal timeout. "I wasn't implying anything. In fact, Mom and Dad are hoping for just the opposite. You should know, they think you and David were made for each other."

Jessie groaned. Covering her face with her hands, she waited a few seconds before spreading her fingers and peeking at her sister. Finally, she dropped her hands.

"Why does your life always seem so simple compared to mine?"

Maria laughed loudly. "Are you crazy? I've got a husband whose work takes him out of town more than I'd like, a young child that wears me out and another one on the way. I can go on."

"You always seem to be in control."

"Maybe I've had time to grow into my situation. You took on a toddler. That's not easy. But then, not many people would do it, either."

Jessie looked down at her uneaten food, unwilling to let her sister see how much she'd come to love Isabel. Like their mother, she knew Maria worried about her getting in too deep.

When she looked up, Jessie said, "I know what you're thinking. But I'm fine. When Elaine comes back, I'll move home and things will get back to normal."

Though Jessie spoke with conviction, her words were hollow. Nothing would ever be normal again. Especially not now, when God had shown her so clearly all that was missing in her life.

Jessie deliberately switched the subject. "When I spoke to Mom yesterday, she said you were feeling really good."

Maria affectionately patted her firm stomach. "Can you believe that? For a while I was afraid the morning sickness would last for the entire pregnancy. I've been bursting with energy. You should see the nursery.''

As Maria launched into a full description of the remodeled nursery, Jessie savored her sister's joy. Without realizing it, her own hand slipped to her stomach as she wondered what it would feel like to trade places with her sister for just one day.

"Oh," Maria exclaimed loudly as she shifted her weight in the chair.

"What is it? Are you okay?" Jessie jumped up and rushed to her sister's side.

"I'm okay. Really. The baby kicked. And I mean, she *kicked*."

Taking Jessie's hand, Maria placed her sister's palm on her taut abdomen. To her disappointment, Jessie felt nothing. Then, just as she started to let go, the unborn baby kicked, and kicked again. Thrilled beyond measure, Jessie shared the special moment with her sister.

Kneeling down, Jessie leaned forward until her lips were mere inches from her sister's stomach. "I'm your aunt Jessie, and I think we're going to get along just fine."

When she stood, she noticed David leaning against the doorjamb. How long had he been watching her?

He quickly moved into the room. "How about that dessert I promised?"

"I think I'm going to have to take a rain check."

With effort, Maria rose. "It's later than I realized. John will be getting worried."

"We understand." David moved with the two sisters toward the front door. "When is your baby due?"

"Not for almost two months. But I have a feeling it's not going to be that long."

"Does the doctor think the baby might come early?" Jessie asked with concern.

"Nope. Just a feeling." A mixture of anticipation and uneasiness darted across Maria's dark eyes.

Jessie hugged her sister. "You take care of yourself."

"I promise." In the doorway Maria turned to David. "We expect to see you and Isabel at the family shower next Sunday. Jessie will give you the details."

When David hesitated, Maria thoughtfully added, "It would mean a lot to the family if you'd join us."

She'd been certain David would tactfully turn down the invitation.

His acceptance shocked her.

As soon as she shut the door behind her sister, she felt her face flush and her voice was filled with disapproval. "What were you thinking when you told my sister you'd go to the lake on Sunday?"

David shrugged, obviously unaware of the blunder he'd just made.

"If you were thinking you'd placate my sister and make an excuse to my mother at the last minute, you can think again. We'll have to meet my family at church, have dinner at my parents' lake house, and then stay for the baby shower. She..." Jessie stopped herself before she said too much. By admitting her mother had matchmaking on her mind, she would only embarrass herself.

David raised his hands in a helpless gesture. "I don't know what I was thinking. If I'd known you'd get so upset, I would have said no."

"Well, if you had glanced my way you'd have known how I felt."

"Hey, I'm sorry. I just couldn't say no to a pregnant woman."

Jessie's mouth opened, but she said nothing. With tears threatening in her eyes, she turned her back to David and rushed from the room.

Halfway down the hallway, he caught her by the elbow and pulled her back to his side. "Forgive me for being so insensitive." When she just looked at him through wide eyes, he added, "I'm not used to having a woman in the house."

He was trying to interject a bit of humor into the dismal moment—she could see that. Even though she didn't find his comment particularly funny, she offered a white-flag smile. "I guess we're both used to making decisions without having to consult anyone. I overreacted."

David continued to hold her loosely by the elbow, despite the fact she showed no signs of running off in mid-sentence. Still, Jessie didn't look into his eyes as she spoke. More than anything, she wanted him to wrap his arms around her and tell her everything would work out. That God had a master plan, and someday, way in the future when she could look back and see how the pieces interlocked, she'd understand God had been with her every step of the way.

"I don't think you overreacted. I can't begin to imagine how hard it is for you."

Lured by the compassion in his voice, Jessie dared to glance at his eyes. With one look, he convinced her he understood completely. He knew that no matter how happy she was for her sister, pain still resided deep inside her heart.

David slipped his arms around Jessie and hugged her. She tried to tell herself it was a friendly hug, a hug of encouragement. But as David's arms lingered, it became harder and harder to convince herself otherwise.

Chapter Thirteen

Ever since Maria's unannounced visit, they'd been snipping and snarling at each other. And Jessie didn't like it. However, it was better than the alternative. At least this way, they kept a safe distance from one another, she realized as they rode in silence to the small church south of Springfield. By the time they'd settled Isabel in the nursery, and she and David entered the sanctuary, the service had begun.

As they waited in the foyer for the minister to finish praying, Jessie inhaled deeply. Her mother turned and, spotting them, waved. Jessie's hopes to slip into a back pew were dashed. Now that her mother had seen them, they had no choice but to proceed to the front of the church. Using the "Amen" as their cue, they walked up the center aisle to the seats her family had saved.

Halfway up the aisle, David casually placed his hand on the small of her back. Her first instinct was to increase her pace—to out-walk his touch, but as she felt the glances and curious stares of her church family she realized resistance would be futile. Friends and family had already assumed she and David were a couple.

Sliding in beside her parents, Jessie tried to focus on the service. But she could think only of the man sitting next to her on the crowded pew. With her side shoved against his, she felt his every movement. When he repositioned his arm, resting it along her shoulders, she glanced at him and he tilted his head in apology. Even though comfort motivated the intimate gesture, she silently admitted that she liked the closeness.

The harder she tried not to think about David, the more she thought about him. She studied his shiny leather shoes, the narrow cuff of his suit pants and the confident way his long fingers spread across his thigh. With every breath she inhaled his fresh, spicy scent, and she savored his deep voice as he sang the hymns. The sermon passed her by in a wordy haze.

But near the end, the minister's voice dropped dramatically in volume. The unexpected whisper caught her attention as she heard him say, ''So many times, we wait for God to call out to us over a loudspeaker and tell us His plans for our lives. And sometimes His way is obvious. But for the most

part, life doesn't work like that. One moment—"
The minister raised one hand with his thumb and
index fingers pinched closely together. "One tiny
moment can change our lives forever."

Jessie's thoughts instantly returned to the night of
the tornado. From that moment on, her life had
never been the same.

Regardless of what happened between her and
David, their meeting had been no accident. Isabel
had awakened her old dream for a family. And while
she really couldn't speak for David, she sensed that
knowing her had helped him move on with his life
and to reopen the lines of communication with God.

Overwhelmed by gratefulness, both to God and
David, Jessie glanced up at the man beside her, only
to find his gaze upon her. He, too, must have realized their meeting on that stormy afternoon had been
no accident.

But where did that leave them now?

When David entered the Claybrook home near
Table Rock Lake, he glanced around the room and
realized he knew quite a few of the guests. And
many of those whom he didn't know, at least had
familiar faces. Springfield was a city with small-
town heart. A city where, if you lived in it long
enough, you got to know just about everyone. And
those you didn't know were related to or acquaintances of those you did know.

With Isabel on his hip, he crossed the living room, wondering if Jessie had been right. He shouldn't have come. And yet, despite the enthusiastic and warm greetings from the Claybrooks and their friends, he still felt out of place.

This wasn't his family.

But Isabel obviously didn't share his reservations. Within minutes she squirmed until he set her down. And then she scurried across the room to where Maria's son, Kraig, played on a quilt that had been spread on the floor in a quieter corner of the room. For a moment, Kraig stopped stacking the bright-colored blocks and stared at Isabel. David realized his daughter's intentions a second too late, and before he could swoop down and pick her up, she reached out her hand, knocked the stack of blocks over and giggled. Kraig just stared at her, then started rebuilding.

Maria appeared at his side. "They'll be fine."

"Isabel's not quite old enough to understand what it means to be a good playmate."

"She'll learn." Maria spoke with a conviction David envied. He constantly worried he wasn't doing a good job of raising his daughter. That he wasn't teaching her all the things he should. No matter how many how-to books he read on child rearing, he never had enough answers.

"Look." Maria pointed to Isabel and Kraig.

Though sitting side by side, they were both playing with separate toys.

"They're happy to hang out with someone their own size."

"Exactly." Before Maria could continue the conversation, someone called to her from across the room and she slipped away.

As David watched his daughter and her new friend, he thought of how he enjoyed spending time with Jessie. It didn't matter whether they were baking bread or listening to jazz CDs or watching Isabel sleep—hanging out with someone he shared common interests and beliefs with, made him feel good about his world.

For the next few hours, David found himself at Jessie's side only briefly. And though he enjoyed conversations with Mr. Claybrook and Jessie's brothers-in-law, he never lost sight of Jessie. Careful to not openly stare at her, he noted her every movement from dinner through the family baby shower.

He marveled at the way she played with her nieces and nephews, the generous hug she bestowed on her very pregnant sister, and the smile that never faded, despite the fact she was at a baby shower. She loved her family, and she was a woman who should have been blessed with a large family of her own. Though he knew Jessie considered that dream impossible, David believed otherwise. Some lucky man would come along and fall head over heels in love with her. It wouldn't matter that she couldn't bear their biological children. She'd find a man who loved her enough to adopt a family.

As much as he loved Isabel, he knew he could love an adopted child. And maybe he would in the future. He didn't want Isabel to grow up without brothers and sisters. There was much more to loving a child than biology.

David stopped cold, gripping the glass of iced tea Jessie's mother had handed him a few minutes ago. What was he thinking? Adopting a child? He couldn't follow these thoughts to their conclusion because he knew where they were headed, and it just wasn't going to happen. He and Jessie were not destined to spend forever together. Forever didn't exist. He'd learned that the hard way.

Still, he couldn't help but glance at her as she regaled her family with a cherished story. With all eyes upon her, he gazed at her unabashedly. Her loving smile, blushed cheeks and bright eyes illuminated her face with a captivating joy.

He admired the way she'd faced her deep disappointment without turning away from God. He admired the way she revealed her love for her family. He admired the way she cared for his daughter. If he ever fell in love again—which he doubted he would—Jessie was the type of woman he wanted to fall in love with.

Then Jessie looked at him—directly into his

soul—and he wondered how he was ever going to find the strength to say goodbye.

Jessie had caught David watching her on several occasions, but she remained determined not to read too much into his furtive glances. Most likely, he felt awkward and out of place among her boisterous family and he hoped she'd give the cue that they'd done their time and could leave.

However, she was in no hurry to go.

She'd missed spending time with family. Today, for reasons she couldn't explain, she appreciated them more than ever.

Her family loved and accepted her for who she was. This was a lesson she needed to take to heart.

Despite her love for her sister, she hadn't looked forward to the baby shower. But with her family's support, she'd faced the event with grace. She didn't want to miss a moment of Maria's happiness. Surprisingly, there'd only been a few fleeting pangs as her sister opened a mound of beautiful gifts. But they were replaced quickly by a confidence that could only have come from God. Although her life had changed direction, God hadn't deserted her. He had special plans for her.

"I hear you're going to be interviewed for an article," Jessie's father announced, after friends had left and only family remained.

"I can't believe you didn't tell us the good

news.'' Maria stopped stacking the pile of new baby clothes.

"It's your day.'' Caught in the spotlight, Jessie suddenly felt uncomfortable.

David jumped in quickly. "It's a tremendous honor and one that's long overdue.''

The admiration in his voice didn't go unnoticed by Jessie.

"When will the article be out?''

"Will you be on the cover?''

"Do you think you'll be interviewed on television, too?''

Family members showed their excitement by firing question after question. By the time Jessie sought out David's gaze, he had disappeared into another room. Oddly, in the midst of her family, she suddenly felt alone.

Instinctively, she checked on Isabel. The toddler waddled toward her, a huge grin on her face. But with her focus on Jessie, Isabel never saw the plastic train, and before Jessie could reach her, Isabel stumbled on the toy and fell backward, hitting her head on the rounded corner of the coffee table.

As she fell to the floor, her scream pierced the room. Jessie hurried to her and inspected her for injury. Satisfied the child was more shocked than hurt, Jessie cuddled her.

From out of nowhere, David appeared to rescue his daughter. Isabel took one look at her father and then pressed her teary face against the side of Jessie's neck, hanging on so tightly Jessie feared the child would leave red marks.

In that moment, Jessie knew she couldn't love Isabel more if she'd given birth to the child. And that was what God had been trying to tell her all along. She wasn't an incomplete woman. God had blessed her with an abundance of love. She'd used not being able to find a husband willing to adopt as an excuse. The truth was, she'd been afraid she'd be incapable of loving and nurturing a child. Thanks to Isabel, those doubts no longer existed.

As if God had knocked a boulder from her shoulders, Jessie felt the emotional weight lift. She no longer feared the future.

However, her joy was short-lived. One look into David's eyes and she could no longer deny she loved this man and his daughter. However, they didn't belong to her, and David had made his intentions clear. What she had with Isabel and David was pretend, and now that God had imparted His lesson, it was time to let them go. It would be selfish of her to stay with Isabel, letting the child become more and more attached.

She knew what she had to do. Squeezing Isabel tightly, Jessie prayed for the courage and the strength to say goodbye.

As lightning cracked across the rainy sky, David closed the nursery blind. Then, tucking his daughter safely into bed, he softly hummed a lullaby his own mother had sung to him and his sister. Without a fight, Isabel sighed loudly, letting her heavy eyelids close.

For a long time he stood at his daughter's side, watching her breathe, praying God would protect her soul through the night.

"Lord, for now help me to be all she needs," he whispered.

Though he couldn't see Jessie, he knew she waited for him in the living room. When they'd returned from her parent's home, she'd said they had to talk. But they really didn't. He already knew what she would say. She'd decided to leave.

He swallowed hard. Reaching down, he gently stroked Isabel's tiny hand. His daughter needed a mother. No, she *deserved* a mother. Jessie had proved that. And even though he had feelings for Jessie, he couldn't bring himself to risk his heart. Perhaps, if the risk involved only himself, he would give love another try. But he had his daughter to think of, and he wouldn't do that to Isabel. They couldn't survive that kind of loss again.

"I know you're too young to understand," he continued to whisper. "Someday, I'll try to explain everything to you."

Leaning forward, he kissed Isabel on the forehead, then he went to find Jessie.

When she wasn't in the living room, he searched the house, calling her name but hearing no answer. Checking the garage and the nanny's quarters, he was relieved to find her car and her clothes and Bible still in place, and since her computer still occupied the living room table he assumed she hadn't gone far.

The lightning flashed again, and when it did he caught a glimpse of her through the living room window. She stood on the front porch, without a coat, her arms crossed. Even from this distance, he could see her shake in the dim light.

With the next flash of lightning, his mind jumped back in time to the night he'd held her in his arms beneath the highway overpass. Pelted by wind, flying gravel and hail, they'd turned to each other for strength. And when he hadn't been able to hold on any longer, she had fought for Isabel as a mother would.

Yes, God had sent him an angel, an answer to his prayers. But from the beginning he'd known she'd only come to him for a short time. She'd come to extend him a hand, to help him come back to the life he'd turned his back on. For that he would always be grateful. For that he would always love her.

But now he had to say goodbye. Jessie needed to go back to her life, and he would move on with his.

He grabbed his long, navy dress coat from the closet, then stepped onto the covered porch. Though she didn't speak, she moved forward, letting him know she was aware of his presence. Around them, lightning lit up the hazy sky as water poured off the gabled roof, surrounding them on three sides with a curtain of rain.

David placed the coat over Jessie's shoulders, and when she didn't resist his touch, he closed his arms around her. With her back pressed against his chest, he attempted to warm her.

"You shouldn't be out here," he said.

"I wanted to see the sky."

Though he heard her voice clearly, she sounded as if she were a million miles away. Desperate to bring her back to him, he tightened his embrace. Even if he couldn't hold on to her forever, he wanted her close for just this moment.

"I have to go," Jessie said.

"I know."

And though he agreed, David suddenly couldn't imagine the day without her. She wouldn't be in the kitchen when he made his morning coffee. Her enchanting fragrance wouldn't greet him at the front door each afternoon when he came home from work. There would be no more prayers, smiles or private jokes shared across the dinner table, nor would he watch her work on the computer until late at night.

"What we feel isn't real," Jessie insisted.

"You're right." Though he agreed, he wondered

if she was right. But either way, her explanation allowed them both a sensible exit.

He squeezed her shoulders tightly. "I can't ever thank you enough for the care you've given Isabel. You've been a lifesaver."

"It was my pleasure. I received much more than I gave."

"Yeah, she has a way of doing that."

"I'd like to see her again...." Jessie stumbled over the words. "I'd love to baby-sit. But I don't think I should see her for a while. It would be too confusing...for her."

Until now, David had been so wrapped up in his own feelings that he hadn't considered how difficult leaving Isabel would be for Jessie. Even though Jessie had been in his house only a short time, her love for Isabel ran deep and true.

"I'd like for Isabel to know you. She needs a woman's influence. But I agree. It would be wise if you didn't spend time with her for a while." David's voice began to shake, but he blamed the trembling on the cold, damp air.

"Maybe by the end of the summer," Jessie suggested.

"The end of summer sounds great." Despite the promise, David knew he wouldn't call Jessie. He couldn't. The break had to be final.

She'd blown into his life, and her exit should be as swift. Without meaning to, he'd become dependent upon her. At times, he'd even taken her presence for granted. He'd missed the companionship of a wife. He'd missed being a whole family. That's all.

He wasn't in love with Jessie.

He'd merely been seduced by the idea of having a family again.

"Who will watch Isabel?" Jessie asked.

"I'm going to take Isabel to the office with me for the rest of the week."

"You won't get much done."

"That's not your worry. But to ease your mind, I talked to Elaine just before I came outside, and she'll be back the first of next week."

"Her sister's doing well, then. That's great news."

"Yeah. Plus, Mom and Dad are on their way home."

The silence stretched between them until lightning struck again.

"I'm sure your employees will be glad to see you in the office full time." David tried to sound optimistic.

Jessie nodded her head and sighed. "I've got a lot to catch up on."

The enthusiasm in her voice sounded forced and brittle.

"Me, too," he said.

Turning in his arms, Jessie looked up at his face. "I think I'll go in now."

He nodded, and when she didn't move, neither did he. Why was it so hard to say goodbye? He decided to focus on all the good she'd brought to his life. Because of Jessie, he'd been reminded there was more to life than just work and his daughter. The best gift he could give Isabel would be to live his life fully. And that included a relationship with God.

Even in the dim light, Jessie's eyes mesmerized him. But he didn't trust himself to read correctly the emotion she tried to hide. Did he see love, or just regret? Was her sorrow tempered by an eagerness to move on?

Unable to let the moment pass, David sensed there was only one way to know her true feelings. Leaning forward, he lowered his lips until he felt Jessie's soft mouth against his. Plagued by uncertainty, he kissed her tentatively. Then her body shifted as she raised her arms to embrace him fully. His coat fell from her shoulders to the porch floor.

Around them, thunder boomed as they gave in to the love they had denied for too long. Oblivious to the rain, damp air and lightning, they didn't part until forced to breathe.

Then, before David could say anything, Jessie ran into the house. He knew he should stop her, go after her. But he didn't. The kiss had told him exactly what he feared.

He did love her.

Shoving his hands into his pants pockets, he hung his head. He wasn't ready to trust in love yet.

He counted three lightning flashes before the garage door opened. Jessie backed her car onto the street and out of his life. As she accelerated, he waved goodbye.

The chilly air penetrated his skin. Still, a long time passed before he went inside to check on his sleeping daughter.

For hours he paced the house, undoing everything Jessie had changed. He stored new flower arrangements and pictures in the hall closet along with a pile of sofa pillows, a new skillet and a stack of CDs he could no longer bear to listen to.

But it didn't work. He couldn't wash her spirit from the house because she had made a home in his heart.

"Oh, God," he prayed, "what am I supposed to do?"

Deep in his heart, he knew he'd made a terrible mistake. But some fences couldn't be mended.

Chapter Fourteen

When Jessie heard the persistent knock at the front door, she groaned. Wearing an old bathrobe and no makeup, she hurried to answer. The last thing she wanted at this early hour was to talk to anyone before she'd had her first cup of coffee. And on this particular morning, she'd need a triple-strength espresso to tackle the headache that threatened to split her skull in half.

"I'm coming. I'm coming," she muttered as she unlocked the dead bolt and opened the door.

"Good morning."

Despite the crisp greeting, compassion softened David's brown eyes. Hope instantly grew in Jessie's heart. Self-consciously, she tightened the robe belt and smoothed stray strands of hair into place. He'd come to his senses. He'd realized he'd made a mistake letting her leave. He wanted her to come *home.*

Overjoyed, Jessie started to jump into his arms. But when she moved forward, she kicked a large object. Looking down, she noticed her suitcases amidst a stack of cardboard boxes—and reality came rushing back.

For a second, she considered telling David she would marry him to become Isabel's mother. That he didn't have to love her. But she knew the compromise would never be enough for her.

"Your things." David's voice remained business-like, though he refused to meet her gaze.

Needing a second to compose herself, Jessie picked up the suitcases and carried them inside the house. With her back to David, she fought to control her emotions. She couldn't let him see her disappointment. Finding strength in the knowledge that moving out of David's house had been the right decision for her and for Isabel, she held her head high. When she faced him, her face betrayed no trace of the love she felt for him.

Hiding behind silence, David carried the boxes into her study, then paused at the front door. Swallowing hard, he glanced at her briefly.

"Thanks for returning my things." Jessie flexed her fingers in an attempt to squelch her desire to reach out and grab hold of his arm, to beg him to reconsider. *We are right together,* she longed to say. *We could be a happy family.*

Instead of speaking to David, she turned her

thoughts into prayer. *Is this Your will, Lord? Should I let him walk out the door?*

Confused, Jessie searched her heart for direction. When she found none, she relied on cold rationalization. David had spoken from his heart on the front porch. Living in close proximity had fooled them into thinking they could be a family. But he didn't love her. And she didn't want a man who didn't love her enough to fight for her.

She saw David swallow hard, then bite down on his bottom lip.

"I'll see you around, Jessie."

"Yeah," she said.

As she closed the door, she knew it would take a long, long time to get over David Akers.

"Why, God? Why didn't this work out?"

With her back pressed against the wall, Jessie slowly eased to the floor, tears following her descent. David hadn't left with just her heart—he'd taken her hopes and dreams of ever having a family with him.

During the following week, Jessie had only one plan—to work each day until she was so tired she fell asleep the instant she crawled into bed. But even though she slept, she dreamed of David. And it was always the same dream. He stood on a high mountain on the far side of a river filled with rapids, calling out her name. Even though she reached for his outstretched hand, the icy water was too swift and dangerous for her to cross.

Shivering and drenched in sweat, Jessie awakened from the terrifying dream. No matter how hard she prayed, peace eluded her.

So she did the only thing she could do. She spent time with her family and she worked until her employees told her to go home.

However, work that she'd once enjoyed, work that had once brought her solace, no longer satisfied her. Instead, it reminded her of what she didn't have and what she had little hope of ever finding. Every time she checked the Web site and saw the many engagement and wedding photos of happy couples, her body stiffened.

When a national department store approached Gifts of Love because they were interested in linking their Internet site to Gifts of Love's bridal registry service, she delegated the negotiations to a trusted employee. Words reminding her of weddings and anniversaries constantly bombarded her. If she had to listen to one more honeymoon, wedding portrait or florist story, she knew she'd scream.

One thought got her through the day—time would heal her broken heart. If she could get through just one more day, the pain would be a little less the next. Still, at this rate, she figured it'd take a lifetime—maybe even two—before her heart quit whispering David's name.

* * *

David put his hands over his head and tried to block out his daughter's cries. For over an hour he'd tried to appease her with soothing songs, ice cream cones and endless rocking, but nothing brought a smile to Isabel's face. Nothing stifled the sad moans that pierced David's heart.

Buckling a pouting Isabel into her car seat, David drove around Springfield for an hour. Zigzagging the city, he kept up an endless flow of senseless chatter, pointing out spots of interest—the Battlefield Shopping Mall, the library, and the Pro Bass Shop that fishermen from around the country visited. He made a silly song up with the names of the main streets—Chestnut, Walnut, Sunshine and Kansas Expressway.

As a last resort he drove an hour south to Branson, and got stuck in the traffic of the burgeoning city that boasted the largest number of country music shows.

"When you get a little bit older, I'll take you to Silver Dollar City. You'll love the rides, the music and the old-time crafts," David promised.

By the time Isabel finally fell asleep, David's nerves had snapped and they were fifty miles from Springfield. On the way home, he passed the highway overpass where he'd held Jessie through the tornado. His heart skipped a beat, and before he knew it, he found himself parked in front of her contemporary brick house. He doubted she would be home in the middle of the day. Yet, when she didn't appear in the window, peeking through a parted curtain, disappointment overwhelmed him.

Why did he have to have met her now? Why couldn't their paths have crossed in five years, when he might be willing to give love another try? Turning slightly, he glanced back at his sleeping daughter. One look convinced him he'd done the right thing. He couldn't risk her innocent heart for his own selfish desires.

Putting the car in gear, David drove down the road, all the while keeping on eye on the rearview mirror, just in case Jessie rushed down the sidewalk waving her arms.

A mile from home, Isabel woke up, and though she wasn't smiling, at least she'd stopped crying. "Hey, Pumpkin, how about we swing by Hot & Fresh and Daddy buys you a cherry strudel?"

Though he was careful not to load Isabel's diet with sweets, his daughter had already acquired a taste for the rich cherry filling.

Carrying Isabel, David walked into the deli and coffee shop, where his employees greeted him with enthusiastic smiles. In an instant, he felt comfortable.

Though it had taken more than a year, he now considered Springfield home. And while he still missed the fast-paced life he'd known in Florida, he'd come to savor the nuances of living in a smaller town.

"We'd like a cherry strudel and a carton of milk," he told the clerk.

While he waited for the order, an older woman he didn't recognize approached him. Walking slowly with a cane, she stopped within inches of Isabel and held out a bony finger to the child.

"Hi there, Miss Isabel," the woman said. "I've heard you're quite the charmer, and you're cute to boot."

"I'm sorry, I don't think we've met." David angled his body to distance Isabel from the woman. He hated feeling suspect of a friendly greeting.

"I sat behind you and Jessie in church a few Sundays ago. I've known her since she and her sisters were little. They used to be in my Sunday School class." The woman winked. "Between you and me, Jessie Claybrook was a handful."

"She still is." Oddly, David enjoyed the lighthearted exchange.

"I expect you'll visit her at the hospital tonight."

David's blood pressure plummeted and his mouth went dry. "What's wrong with her?"

"That I don't know. An emergency call went out through our prayer chain a few hours ago. All I know is that Jessie was taken to the hospital and that she's in serious condition."

The news stunned David, and for a moment every

muscle in his body froze. If someone had yelled "Fire!" he wouldn't have been able to run.

Without warning, he found himself jolted back in time to another horrible moment. He'd been standing in one of his Miami restaurants when the police team came to tell him his wife had been in a serious accident. For an eternity, he'd sat by her hospital bed and begged God to save her life.

Then suddenly, he saw images of Jessie. He saw her wearing a wedding dress. He saw her wading in Table Rock Lake with Isabel. He saw her holding a newly adopted baby. He saw her looking up at him and smiling.

The choice was his. When he'd lost his wife, the circumstances had been beyond his control. But if he lost Jessie, he could blame only himself.

Isabel's shrieks jerked him back to the present. Unaware he'd squeezed his daughter too tightly, he whispered apologies in her ear.

"You don't know any more details?"

Resting the majority of her weight on a wooden cane, the woman shook her head.

"Please, think hard."

With pursed lips, the woman continued to shake her head.

From behind the counter the young clerk announced their order was ready.

"There's been a change of plans," he shouted as he raced for the door, got in his car and drove straight to the hospital as fast as he could without risking his daughter's life. He jumped out of the car and, holding Isabel tightly, he ran across the parking lot.

"Please, God, keep her safe. Don't let anything happen to our Jessie."

By the time he reached the main entrance, he gasped for breath. Not willing to rest for even a second, he barged into the hospital and went directly to the information desk.

"Can you tell me which room Jessie Claybrook is in?"

While David impatiently shifted his weight from one foot to the other, the volunteer typed Jessie's name into the computer. When the bald man scratched his head, typed another line and then waited, dread blanketed David.

"I'm sorry, Jessie Claybrook isn't a patient here."

"No, she has to be," David insisted. "Look again. Please."

With calm dignity, the gentleman said, "I've already looked twice. There's no Jessie Claybrook listed. Perhaps you've gotten her name wrong or maybe she's in another hospital."

"Of course," David said. Because she lived and worked on the south side of Springfield, he'd automatically assumed this is where they'd taken her.

But if she'd become ill in another part of the city, it was likely she'd been admitted to another facility.

"Do you have the number of the other hospitals?"

As if he'd done this before, the man quickly supplied a sheet with the telephone numbers and addresses of area medical clinics and hospitals.

David called every single number on the list.

With disbelief, he snapped his telephone shut. No one had a Jessie Claybrook listed.

"Where are you, Jessie?" he said out loud.

Could the woman who'd heard the news through her church prayer chain have been mistaken? No, he didn't think so. The concern in her eyes had been real. And the fear invading his heart compelled him to keep searching.

He had to find Jessie.

He had to see for himself that she was all right.

Too upset to think rationally, David paced across the narrow entryway as he tried to clear his mind so he could decide where to look next.

From somewhere came the urge to go to the chapel and pray. At first he resisted, thinking he needed to be looking, not sitting somewhere while he lost Jessie. Finally, the prompting became so strong he couldn't ignore it. He needed God.

Rushing past the volunteer desk, with Isabel in his arms, David followed the signs to the chapel. He paused outside the door and took a deep breath, then entered the holy quietness. With his head bowed he stood in the back of the dimly lit sanctuary.

He didn't look up until Isabel raised her finger and pointed. "Mama, mama, mama."

A slender woman knelt at the altar. Before she turned around, he knew. He'd found Jessie.

Rushing toward her, he and Isabel met her in the aisle, and the three embraced as they had beneath the highway overpass.

Now that he'd found Jessie, he was never going to let her go.

Jessie couldn't believe her eyes.

"Is it really you?" she asked, as David blotted the tears from her cheeks with his fingers.

David nodded. "Are you okay?"

"I'm fine. But why are you here? How did you know where to find me?" While she was glad to see him, his sudden appearance confused her.

"God sent us to you. Just like he sent you to us that night on the highway."

Overwhelmed, Jessie began to sob. With patience, David let her lean against him until she regained her composure.

"It's Maria."

"The elderly woman had you confused with your sister."

Jessie didn't know what David was talking about, and she didn't care. "Maria's gone into labor—too soon. There are complications. The doctors don't know—if she's going to—make it." Jessie pushed the words off her tongue in short staccato bursts.

Taking her hand in his, David lifted her fingers to his lips. "We have to have faith and believe she's going to be okay."

Knowing all he'd suffered through with his late wife, Jessie appreciated how difficult it must be for David to encourage her. It also proved to her that he'd turned back to God.

"I do believe," she said. "But I feel so guilty."

"Why?" David asked.

Isabel, impatient with the conversation, reached out her tiny hands to Jessie, and Jessie welcomed the child into her arms. As she hugged Isabel tightly, she tried to explain.

"I've wasted so much time envying my sisters' families."

"You never wished them harm. You're not to blame for what's happening to Maria."

"Rationally, I know that. Yet for so long, I've blamed God for my inability to bear children. I was so angry I convinced myself I'd never find a man who would want to marry me and adopt a family, when the honest truth was that I really believed God had caused me to be barren because I would never be a good mother."

"Oh, Jessie," David said with great compassion.

She kissed Isabel on the forehead and then rubbed

noses with the little girl. "But this little one has changed me. God brought her into my life to show me I have the love of a mother, and someday when I get married, I'm going to adopt a house full of children."

"I believe you will."

Sensing he wanted to say something more, she waited.

Finally he said, "We need to talk, but not until we know Maria is okay."

Taking Jessie's hand, David led her and Isabel back to the front altar. They kneeled together, and David prayed.

"Dear Lord, we don't always understand Your ways, but we know You love us and care for us. In Your great love, we ask You to watch over Maria and her unborn child. We ask You to comfort her and to help her deliver a healthy baby. And we ask that You will restore health to both mother and child."

Comforted by the prayer and by David's arm resting across her shoulders, Jessie placed her worries and fears in God's hands. She didn't resist when David pulled her closer. Letting her head rest against his collar bone, she continued to pray for her sister.

Nearly half an hour had passed when she heard the creak of the door. Continuing to pray, neither Jessie nor David turned to look at the intruder, until Jessie felt a tap on her shoulder.

When she turned around, she saw her mother's tear-stained face. Her heart sank.

Then a smile dawned on Helene's face. "Maria's turned a corner. She's doing much better. She's going to be okay. And she has a beautiful baby daughter. She's small, but healthy."

"Oh, Mom," Jessie exclaimed. As she fell into her mother's embrace, she thanked God for answering her prayers.

"What good news!" David exclaimed.

Over her daughter's shoulder, Helene said, "I'm glad you've been here with Jessie."

"There's nowhere else I ever want to be."

Uncertain she'd heard David correctly, Jessie slowly turned her head. When she finally met his gaze, she saw that love filled his eyes. Confused, Jessie glanced away.

Oblivious to the exchange between Jessie and David, Helene tugged on her daughter's arm, motioning them to follow her. "The baby's already in the nursery."

Jessie sighed with thanks for the timely diversion.

A few minutes later, they all stood in front of the nursery window. Isabel, balanced on Jessie's hip, found the room full of babies fascinating, and immediately patted her hand against the window.

"There's my precious granddaughter," Helene said.

"Ooh." Jessie gazed at the dark-haired newborn her mother pointed to. "She's so beautiful."

"God's gift," Helene whispered.

Tears filled Jessie's eyes as she studied the little miracle. With hesitation David stepped behind her, resting his hands lightly on her shoulders, as if he wasn't certain Jessie would let him share the tender moment with her. To ease his fears, Jessie reached up and squeezed his hand.

Attuned to the intimacy, Helene opened her arms to Isabel and took the child from Jessie. "Let's give your Daddy and Jessie some time to themselves."

David waited until Helene and Isabel had disappeared through the doorway. Sliding his fingers slowly down the side of Jessie's face, he seemed too emotional to speak.

To break the awkward silence, Jessie said, "I want to thank you again for being here with me. I don't know what I would have done if—"

David rubbed her earlobe between his fingers. "Shh. Your sister is going to be fine, and your niece is healthy and radiant." Pausing as if to gather his courage, David added, "I needed you, too."

Jessie looked deep into his eyes and knew she'd found the man she'd love for the rest of her life.

David sighed, shutting his eyes for a moment. "When the woman came into the store and said you were in the hospital, I thought I was going to die. The possibility of losing you scared me to my senses." With his hands on both her shoulders, David's gaze remained focused on her. "Can you forgive me for letting my fears and bitterness and anger toward God come between us? Not loving you is the biggest risk I could ever take."

Tears gathered in Jessie's eyes and her voice temporarily deserted her. She nodded, then finally managed to say the words. "I love you, David. I think I have from the first moment we huddled under the overpass."

David bit down hard on his bottom lip, as if what he'd just heard was too good to believe. "Will you marry me? Will you share your life with me and Isabel?"

Jessie immediately threw her arms around David's neck and shouted, "Yes…yes…yes. I'll be your wife."

Nestled in his arms, Jessie basked in the warmth and hope of love. Though the moment would end, she knew their love never would.

Lost in the awareness of one another, neither realized a woman had joined them at the nursery window. "Which baby is yours?" she quietly asked.

Both Jessie and David turned to look at the petite woman in the dark navy suit and sensible shoes.

"It's my sister's baby," Jessie quickly corrected.

"Our niece," David added.

Our niece. She liked the way he'd said that, as if they'd always been family.

"Forgive the mistake. You just looked so happy and in love. And the way you were looking at the babies...well..."

"No offense taken. We are in love," David said.

Jessie's body stiffened and she tried to ease from David's arms. But before she could break free, he tightened his embrace, pulling her close to him.

Still, the moment had been tarnished. How could she have been so shortsighted? She and David had never discussed the issue of adoption. Until moments ago, when he'd asked her to marry him, there hadn't been any need to. He'd already told her he'd always planned to have a large family.

David's arms tightened again, as if he felt her doubts.

To the woman he said, "Jessie just said she'd marry me. And we'll be adopting a child as soon as we can."

Looking up at David, the glow in his eyes stunned her. He'd meant every word.

"That's fantastic." Honest joy radiated from the woman's face. "And forgive me for not introducing myself, but I'm Dorothy Thompson with the James Adoption Agency. I'm here checking on a baby that was born this morning and is being adopted through our agency. If you're really serious about adoption, let me give you a card. I'd love to meet with you."

Still at a loss for words, Jessie smiled and nodded,

as David accepted Ms. Thompson's business card and shook her hand.

"Are you sure about this?" Jessie asked as soon as the woman disappeared from their sight.

"I've never been more certain about anything in my life."

Jessie felt she needed to be blunt. "I can't give birth to your child."

With a gentle caress, David pushed a strand of hair behind her ear. "I understand. This wasn't a decision I made lightly."

Even though it had been a blessing to meet Ms. Thompson at this particular moment, Jessie knew adoption wasn't always an easy process. Sometimes couples waited a year or more before they were matched with an infant.

Turning Jessie's body slightly, he made her face the nursery. "It wasn't until I saw all these babies and my heart swelled with love that I knew. I could take any one of them home and raise them as my own."

"You're sure?" Jessie said again, giving him a chance to change his mind.

"Why is this so hard for you to accept? You love Isabel as if she's your own, don't you?"

Jessie nodded.

"Don't you think I'm capable of doing the same?"

"Oh, yes." And more. They had their whole future ahead to discover the depths of their love.

"I'm glad that's settled. You, me and Isabel—we're a family," David said. "Now, we've got a wedding and an adoption to plan."

With fingers entwined, Jessie and David walked a few steps before they both turned around to gaze one last time at the nursery. Hot tears of joy streamed down Jessie's face as she realized how one special moment had changed her life forever.

Epilogue

As soon as Jessie and David walked into their house, a loud cheer exploded. Grandparents, brothers, sisters, nieces and nephews had gathered to celebrate the latest addition to the Akers and Claybrook families.

A large, colorful banner stretched from one side of the living room to the other: Welcome Home, Levi.

"Well, where is my newest grandson?" Helene Claybrook asked. Moving to Jessie's side, she waited impatiently while Jessie pulled the blanket away from the precious bundle in her arms.

Fully exposing his rosy cheeks, Jessie held her new son up for everyone to see. "I'd like you all to meet Levi."

Oohs and aahs were followed by tender smiles as every family member stepped forward to greet Levi.

Leaning down, David planted a kiss on Jessie's temple. "Did you ever dream we'd be so blessed?"

Jessie smiled as she shook her head.

Behind her, she heard four-year-old Isabel explaining her version of Levi's adoption to her cousins.

"You see, Levi is only three days old and we got to pick him out from all the babies in the hospital and bring him home." Then she tugged on Jessie's skirt for attention. "Mom, do you think the next time God sends us a baby, you could tell Him we'd like a girl? I'd sure like to have a sister."

Jessie glanced at David, the twinkle in his eyes contagious. Squatting down, he put his hand on Isabel's shoulder and said, "I think God would be happy to send you a sister and maybe even another brother."

Isabel giggled, then wrapped her arms around Jessie's legs. Jessie passed her son to her husband, then, sensing Isabel felt left out because of all the attention Levi was getting, she picked Isabel up and hugged her.

"Tell me a story, Mommy," Isabel whispered.

Jessie's eyes watered. She knew Isabel wanted her to tell the story of how God had tossed Isabel into Jessie's arms during the tornado.

Jessie began. "It was a stormy night and the winds were fierce. You, me and Daddy huddled beneath the highway overpass, praying God would protect us from harm.''

As Jessie spoke, she met David's gaze and silently thanked God for caring enough to give her the most precious gift of all—a family to love.

* * * * *

Dear Reader,

I hope you've enjoyed Jessie and David's story. Like Jessie, I also love to bake bread. Since many of my favorite memories are of my mother, Jozell, teaching me to bake, I thought I'd share with you a family recipe she passed on to me. In fact, my mother once made a thousand potato rolls for a wedding reception!

They're easy and delicious. Enjoy!

All my best,

Crystal Stovall

POTATO ROLLS

1 pkg yeast	1 1/2 tsp salt
1/4 cup water	1 cup scalded milk
1/2 cup hot mashed potatoes	1 egg
1/4 cup shortening	4 to 4 1/2 cups flour
1/4 cup sugar	

Soften yeast in water and set aside. Combine potatoes, shortening, sugar, salt and milk. Cool to lukewarm and add egg and yeast. Stir in 2 cups flour and beat well. Stir in 2-2 1/2 cups flour and knead until smooth and elastic. Place in a greased bowl and let rise until double in bulk. Punch down and form into 24 balls. Place on a greased cookie sheet and let rise until double in size. Bake at 400°F for 10 to 12 minutes. Remove from oven and rub butter on top of rolls. Cool on wire racks.

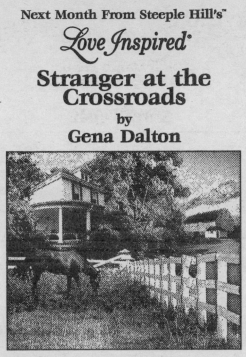

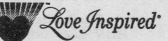

Next Month From Steeple Hill's™

Love Inspired

Hunter's Bride
by
Marta Perry

Thanks to *one* little white lie, Chloe Caldwell's family
believed she was dating her handsome boss, and they'd
just invited Luke Hunter to a family celebration. Chloe
intended to set the record straight. Until Luke handed
her plane tickets for *two*...and it looked as if her
prayers had been answered!

Don't miss
HUNTER'S BRIDE

On sale May 2002

Love Inspired

Visit us at www.steeplehill.com

LIHB